Clever-Lazy

Joan Bodger

Tundra Books

To my husband, Alan Nelson Mercer

Adapted from *Clever-Lazy, The Girl Who Invented Herself*,
originally published in 1979 in Canada by McClelland & Stewart,
and in the United States by Atheneum.

Copyright © 1997 by Joan Bodger

Published in Canada by Tundra Books, *McClelland & Stewart Young Readers*,
481 University Avenue, Toronto, Ontario M5G 2E9

Published in the United States by Tundra Books of Northern New York,
P.O. Box 1030, Plattsburgh, New York 12901

Library of Congress Catalog Number: 97-60507

All rights reserved. The use of any part of this publication reproduced,
transmitted in any form or by any means, electronic, mechanical,
photocopying, recording, or otherwise, or stored in a retrieval system,
without the prior written consent of the publisher - or, in case of
photocopying or other reprographic copying, a licence from the Canadian
Copyright Licensing Agency - is an infringement of the copyright law.

Canadian Cataloguing in Publication Data

Bodger, Joan
   Clever-Lazy

ISBN 0-88776-418-5

I. Title.

PS8553.O44C6 1997   jC813´.54   C97-930718-X
PZ7.B63523Cl 1997

We acknowledge the support of the Canada Council for the Arts for our
publishing program.

Cover illustration: Chum McLeod
Cover design: Sari Ginsberg

Printed and bound in Canada

1 2 3 4 5 6   02 01 00 99 98 97

Contents

Like all good fantasies, this one is based on truth. The setting is not China, but most of the inventions can be found in Joseph Needham's *Science and Civilization in China*. He confirms that the Chinese court valued the inventions as toys, not something to utilize. How Clever-Lazy made fireworks is taken from a volume by a seventeenth-century Polish gentleman. The notion of dragon lines as a force within the earth is worldwide. In China it is called *feng-shui*; in Britain, ley lines; in Australia, song lines.

Business ventures engaged in by Clever-Lazy, Tinker, Bowlmaker, Shopshrewd, and others are to show the romance of trade and the fun of earning one's own way. The old soldier, Scar, comes from my own experience as a sergeant in World War II.

You may recognize bits and pieces from "The Buried Moon" by Joseph Jacobs, and from "The Nightingale" by Hans Christian Andersen. The singing bone motif is universal.

1

The Birth of
Clever-Lazy

FAR AWAY, AND on the other side of time, there lived a baker and a baker's husband. They worked hard every day of the year and made a fair living, but they thought they would be happier if they had a child. So one day Baker said to her husband, "Tomorrow let us close the shop early and go up into the Dancing Mountains to the shrine of the Goddess, and ask her to send us a child. I shall take a gift to her so she will know exactly what we want."

Then the baker woman set about making a baby doll out of dumpling dough, round and soft, full of creases and dimples. She made a girl doll.

The next day wife and man closed the shop early and set off for the shrine. They wore their cloaks because it was cold in the mountains. The man carried a mat for sitting on and the woman carried a basket. Inside the basket was the doll. Wedged around it were little packages of fried rice, pickled herbs and at least a dozen small cakes to keep the doll from being shaken about.

They walked for more than three days, following signs and landmarks and alignments known only to the woman. By the afternoon of the third day, they had to pull themselves up by the roots of gnarled pine trees and help each other clamber through the clefts of great rocks.

By the time they reached the shrine, their hearts were pounding. The niche where the baker said her grandmother had said the Goddess would be was too dark to make out a shape among the shadows. They could hardly see the Goddess, set back as she was in a small cave. The light was further obscured by a tall gray-green boulder, almost like a half-opened door, that stood in front of the cave, casting its own long shadow. The man thought to himself that if it were not for his wife, he would never have guessed that a statue of a goddess was hidden there. But his wife went at once into the space between the boulder and the cave mouth, and flung herself down on a flat lichen-dappled stone. The man knelt a little way behind her. They both waited for the Goddess, unseen in the shadows, to speak to them. Since the Goddess said nothing, Baker opened her basket and took out the doll made of dumpling dough. Then the woman, holding up the doll for the Goddess to see, crawled forward a little.

"O Goddess," she prayed, "please send a girl baby as pretty and plump as this doll made of dumpling dough."

"O Goddess," prayed her husband, from a little way behind her, "Please send us a girl child who will grow up to be as pretty and plump and clever as my wife." Then they quit the shrine, taking the basket but leaving the doll behind them. Neither of them had actually seen the Goddess, but they felt better for having come so far to speak to her.

They looked for a place where they could rest and eat and enjoy the view. The man found an old pine tree that grew near the top of the mountain. In a soft hollow beneath the tree, he spread the mat on a pile of pine needles. The woman sat down on the mat and unpacked the basket. They shared what was left of the rice and herbs, and finished up the cakes. When they were thirsty, they drank from a spring that trickled out of a rhododendron thicket and fell as a waterfall to a hidden plateau below.

Then the man leaned back against the pine tree, and the woman leaned against the man, and they watched the sun set in the west. Then they searched for the first star. Then they watched the new moon. Then they decided that it was late and too dark to go down the mountainside; they had better wait until dawn. And because the night was cold as well as dark, they pulled their cloaks over themselves as blankets, and crept close together to keep each other warm. By the time the night sky was spangled with stars, they were fast asleep.

They did not see the fiery globe that rose from the plateau below them to speed across the heavens. They did not see the dragon ship of the Goddess.

In the morning they awakened when it was still dark because that was the usual time for them to get out of bed and light the ovens. They ate the cake crumbs and drank some water, then started home down the mountainside. The return was much faster than the going, although they did not try to hurry. By the next morning they had come to the fields just above the village. They walked along the familiar path holding hands.

"Everything looks new and different," said the man, astonished.

"Perhaps that's because we've let ourselves be lazy," said his wife. "If we ever have a child," she said, "I hope she will be clever enough to be lazy, and lazy enough to be clever."

But the man's mind was already beginning to think of a thousand chores concerning the house and bakery. Desperately Baker tried to grasp what had seemed so clear to her a moment before. 'There is something I must remember,' she thought. Then, with her husband, she rushed toward the village to begin the day's work.

Did the Goddess hear their prayers? I do not know for sure. However, it came about less than a year later that a baby girl was born to them. She was far prettier than the dumpling doll, dimpled and sweet-tempered from the beginning. They decided to call her "Clever-Lazy."

2

The Childhood of Clever-Lazy

WHEN CLEVER-LAZY WAS a tiny baby, she rode sometimes on her father's back, sometimes on her mother's. While her parents busied themselves about the shop, she peered over one or the other's shoulder with wise eyes that seemed to notice everything. When she was a little older, they spread a mat on the bakery floor so she could crawl. They gave her pot lids to play with, and made a rattle for her by putting beans and peppercorns into a stoppered jar. When she could toddle, they let her play about their feet, opening and closing doors, dragging out cooking pots, crawling into chests and boxes.

"But won't she hurt herself?" asked the neighbors. "Won't she get in the way? Isn't she a nuisance?"

Baker and her husband only laughed or shrugged their shoulders. As soon as Clever-Lazy was able to walk, they took her to the great oven and held her hand on a part that was very warm, but not warm enough to burn her. "Hot," they said, and Clever-Lazy learned to say and know the meaning. She knew, too, by the respect her parents paid to the fire, that what was useful and beautiful could also be dangerous. Long years afterward, she would have occasion to remember that.

In the meantime, she observed that a dancing orange flame would make a kettle sing, that a dull red glow was needed for roasting and baking, that a blue flame was the hottest (although it looks cold), and that great heat could change the color and shape of metals. These things she learned because she was allowed to see.

As for being a nuisance, I suppose Clever-Lazy was often that. But her parents were willing to forgive her because she brought to them such joy and amusement. The first time she pulled a bag of flour down all over herself, they merely laughed and dusted her off. The next time they gave her a pan of flour of her own, and lent her their cups and bowls and spoons so she could pour and measure to her heart's content.

Clever-Lazy amused herself by the hour comparing and sorting little piles of rice and millet, almonds and pista-chios, poppy seeds and sesame. She loved to let their names slide over her tongue almost as much as she liked to let their shapes and colors and textures slide through her fingers. She even made patterns and pictures by sticking nuts and seeds, beans and beads, to panels of wood, which her proud parents hung on the wall of their shop.

Quite early Clever-Lazy learned to count. She arranged and rearranged rows of beads so that her fingers fairly flew as she ordered the numbers. When she was older, she evolved a pattern that enabled her to help her parents calculate how many pounds of flour they would need for the months ahead, what the loss or profit would be if they enriched a recipe or how many days it was before the equinox, when the farmers would plant a new crop. Because the beads rolled away under her flying fingers, she asked her father to make a little rack. Heeding her directions, he helped her thread seven beads onto thirteen spindles, then enclosed them in a frame. Of course neither of them knew that Clever-Lazy had invented the abacus! "Click-click-click," went the beads as Clever-Lazy moved them swiftly up and down.

When the Imperial Tax Collector came to the village, he watched in amazement as Clever-Lazy, sitting companionably beside him, clicked out how much each villager owed the Emperor, far faster and more accurately than he could by adding up a long row of figures with brush and paper, or even by moving counters in a box.

The villagers were not much pleased, but the Emperor's man asked if he could have a similar bead rack of his own. He wanted to show his wife, who long ago had lived in the Province of the Dancing Mountains. Clever-Lazy gave him hers willingly. Her father said he would make her another, but somehow or other he never did. But what happened to that first abacus would one day be important to Clever-Lazy.

Clever-Lazy didn't spend all her time with grown-ups, of course. She ran and played with the other village children as

often as they could get away from their chores. She played
hopscotch and skipped rope and flew kites and played tag
and threw balls and spun tops and ran races and played
hide-and-seek. She told stories while the other children
worked in their gardens or tended the cattle, and she helped
them catch fish in the canals. She even devised a prawn trap
for them.

The prawn trap looked something like a kite, but it was
made of rice sacking stretched tight over a certain kind of
root. The children would set their traps in the morning
(each child had his own dark and secret little current that
he thought best), then at noon they would go back and
haul up the traps, cook the prawns and have a feast. It was
not long before the adults copied the children, and soon
the local market was renowned not only for its prawns,
but for its prawn traps. The village was richer for having
Clever-Lazy in its midst, but I am not prepared to tell you
whether the villagers were grateful. They complained about
her laziness and muttered that she was a bad influence on
their children.

Clever-Lazy liked to mix things together that had never
been mixed together before. She stirred, tasted and tested
her recipes on top of the brazier or in the big oven. Sometimes they tasted good, and sometimes they tasted so bitter
all one could do was to pull a face. Once or twice they
made the whole family ill, and several times her concoctions actually exploded in the oven. Once, when that
happened, Clever-Lazy noticed that the inside of the oven
had lost all its crust of old soot and grease, and looked as

clean as new. By remembering what she had put into her recipe (a little soda, a little lemon juice, a pinch of lye and other things), she was able to make a sort of paste with which her parents could paint the oven. They left the paste on overnight, and the next morning her father washed down the walls and found that the oven was clean again, this time without the bother and danger of an explosion.

"So you see," said her mother to the neighbors, "Clever-Lazy is more help to us than if she spent all of her time learning to do housework."

There were other benefits as well. Who invented poppy seed rolls? Who invented sesame seed bread? Why, Clever-Lazy, of course. And it was Clever-Lazy who made a sort of tea out of the stamens of spring crocus, and persuaded Baker to add it to the dough so that the whole village, and several villages beyond, learned to enjoy yellow saffron buns. Oh yes, and she taught her parents to bury the great long pod of a vanilla bean in the sugar jar so as to flavor all the cakes. And, speaking of cakes, Clever-Lazy it was who first thought to beat egg whites, and thought of adding them to cakes to make them rise in the oven. And it was Clever-Lazy who taught her parents to sift flour through a series of baskets so that the breath of air was added to exceedingly fine flour along with the egg whites. No wonder that Baker's confections were compared to the clouds that could be seen floating over the Dancing Mountains.

Clever-Lazy liked to hear her parents tell the story of how they had made a dumpling dough doll and had gone to the Goddess to ask for a baby. She made dolls of flour and eggs and sugar, too, and found that by adding cornstarch, she could make stiffer figures that lasted indefinitely. She painted faces on them and fashioned clothes and armor. In the evenings, she delighted her parents by telling stories and acting them out with the aid of her puppets made from dough.

Clever-Lazy kept her ever-growing collection of story figures in a box her father made for her, which her mother lined with gold and red paper. The inside of the box was designed to hold three square trays fitted one on top of the other. Each tray was divided into sections to keep her story figures separate and safe. Only the soldiers, dozens of them, were dumped together in a jumble on the bottom. There was a latch on the box and a curved brass handle that made it easy to pick up and carry about. Clever-Lazy painted the box bright red.

Sometimes neighbors came to hear the stories too. And a certain young tinker who came by every few months to mend and sell pots and pans made it his business to spend the night in that particular village just to hear and watch Clever-Lazy tell her stories. He was a lonely young man who traveled the roads most of the year, and who had no family of his own. I dare say if you had asked him his dearest wish, he would have replied that what he really longed for was a home and a family as much like the bakers' as possible. And, if you had asked him why, he would not have been able to answer.

One night when he knocked on the door, he was invited into the household and given a good supper, along with a welcome order for pots and pans. Clever-Lazy had just finished a new play and had cut out and painted a new cast of characters, so she made him especially welcome. She knew that, except for her parents, no one was as entranced by her stories as was young Tinker. He, in return, found it delightful to watch her fuss about, setting up the stage while her mother and father finished the dishes and completed their chores for the morning. If he wondered why she did not help her parents, he might also have noticed that they offered no reprimand or reproof. He soon allowed himself to forget Clever-Lazy's laziness, and to give himself over to enjoying the new play when the rest of the small audience settled down with him.

The new play was far more complicated than Clever-Lazy had ever produced before. There were an Emperor and an Empress, an easily-frightened princess, a dragon, an army (a rather small one), Daunted Knight and Proud Maiden. At first, Tinker thought that Proud Maiden was another knight, or perhaps a soldier, because she was dressed in armor and because she fought and ousted the dragon after Daunted Knight had failed. When he discovered she was a girl, he was quite sure that the knight would marry her if only she would become as docile and grateful as the princess. But that's not the way the story turned out at all. Proud Maiden sent Daunted Knight away and decided to go on to other adventures by herself.

Tinker was unsettled. True, even he had never laughed so much nor followed a plot so breathlessly, but he was left with the uneasy feeling that he would wish some other fate for the knight and the maiden. When Clever-Lazy announced that of all the characters she had ever created, she loved Proud Maiden best by far, Tinker felt an unaccountable pang. "How could a nice girl like you admire a girl like that?" he asked, puzzled. "I don't think she's really respectable."

"What does respectable mean?" asked Clever-Lazy. Tinker would have been scandalized by her ignorance if he had not realized that her not knowing was final proof of respectability. *He* worried about that question most of the time.

"Someone who is respectable does what is expected of her," he replied.

"But that's why I like Proud Maiden best. She does the *unexpected*."

Next day, Tinker hoisted his pack to his back, shook the village dust from his feet and turned his face to the open road. He had never felt so lonely.

3

The Almond Tree

NOW CAME A time when the water in the canals dropped lower and lower, and the crops withered in the fields. The sky overhead was like the inside of a tarnished bowl, dull yet shining, sealing out the rain. The farmers had no grain to take to the mill, and the miller had no flour to sell to the baker. No one thought to buy cakes. It was hard enough to find the price of bread! Baker and her husband talked far into the night about what they should do.

Everyone waited for the snow to fall. Perhaps the snow would heal the land. But that winter, for the first time in living memory, there was no snow. Only a cold and biting wind came to stir the dust, which later froze into tight ridges. In the spring, those few farmers who still had seed planted it with more fear than hope. The whole village prayed for the first sign of green.

The date of Clever-Lazy's birthday came in the spring. Her parents had warned her that there was little they could do to celebrate the occasion of her fifteenth year, but as I have said before, Clever-Lazy was of a sweet and happy disposition. Certainly she was not a greedy child. When they asked her if she could think of anything at all that she would like for her birthday (anything within the realm of possibility, that is), she asked them to take her up into the Dancing Mountains to visit the shrine of the Goddess. All her life they had talked about such a visit, and now she was surely old enough for them to show her the way.

On the morning of her birthday, Clever-Lazy awoke to find the sun shining and a lovely shadow, familiar yet unfamiliar, dancing on the thin paper screen that covered her window. Hardly daring to hope, she pushed back the screen and found that the almond tree that she had thought dead had burst into bloom, covering the branches with blossoms of dazzling white. No other birthday present could have pleased her more. She ran into her parents' room to share the good news, and they, too, came to marvel and to agree with her that surely this must be a good omen. Then her parents packed a meal, albeit much more frugal than the one they had taken with them years before, and they all set out for the mountains.

As they walked through the fields, they rejoiced to see that new crops had poked up thin green blades through the hard earth crust. When they came near the mountains, Baker was careful to point out to Clever-Lazy certain landmarks that she used to guide them. She showed Clever-Lazy how to align one peak or notch or outcropping with another. "This does not happen by chance," she said. "The Goddess has planned it all."

Clever-Lazy was a little dizzy from lack of food, but even so, she fairly danced along. Was this not her birthday? And was she not going to visit the Goddess? She looked at everything with wide open eyes, and impressed every peak and scarp and vale and waterfall upon her mind and heart as though they were on a painted scroll. "This is the most important day of my life," she told herself. "I shall remember this forever."

When they hauled themselves up to the flat place near the mountaintop, Baker and her husband had to rest for a long while and to learn how to breathe in the thin mountain air. Even Clever-Lazy was glad of a rest. Then her mother led Clever-Lazy to the place behind the green rock; the rock that stood like a door ajar in front of the cave. The cave was so shadowed that Clever-Lazy was not at all sure, peering over her mother's shoulder, whether she could actually see the Goddess. What she was aware of was a great stillness, a peaceful strength that seemed to spread out from the darkness. Each of the members of the little family said a prayer. The man asked the Goddess to look after his wife and child. The woman asked the Goddess to add wisdom to her daughter's cleverness. As for Clever-Lazy, she asked the Goddess to make the next year of her life the most exciting yet. After all, she reminded the Goddess, she did not want to be a dumpling doll forever.

Afterward, the three of them hunted for squirrels' stores of last year's pine nuts, and dug for roots to cook and eat. Baker found some watercress near the little stream, and Clever-Lazy and her father searched for mushrooms. The day was a quiet but happy one. When at last they gathered under the pine tree to eat their simple meal, Clever-Lazy asked her parents how they knew about the shrine of the Goddess.

"I know only because your mother knows," said Baker's husband.

"And I know because my grandmother brought me here when I was a girl about your age," said Baker. "She told me long ago that the shrine was tended by priestesses, women who lived in a temple. Indeed, she told me that she and I, and that would mean you, too, Clever-Lazy, were descended from one of the priestesses who was forced to flee when the Great Calamity happened. They had to go into hiding. The palace of the Goddess disappeared below the waters; her shrines were destroyed, neglected and forgotten. Her last few priestesses fled. This is the only shrine remaining."

"Are there no other women who believe in her?" asked Clever-Lazy.

"All over the world there are those who remember her, but they are few and far between. Most dare not speak of her, and none of them know the whereabouts of this place. Only my grandmother knew, and *she* told *me*. The only people I have ever told are your father, whom I trust absolutely, and now you. You and I, my darling Clever-Lazy, are the only women left to tend this shrine. This is the place from whence she flew away."

"Flew away?" asked Clever-Lazy, intrigued. "How did she do that?"

"My grandmother said a dragon came down and picked her up. She flew away on a dragon — or in a dragonship. My grandmother was not sure which."

"But how . . . ?" asked Clever-Lazy.

Her father interrupted. "I don't think we should burden the child with more than it is safe to know," he admonished his wife. "Clever-Lazy, the penalty for speaking of the Goddess is death. I tell you this for your own good."

"But I've heard people speak of her. Not often — but sometimes."

"Here in the Province of Dancing Mountains we are more careless," said her mother. "For one thing, this was the last known place where the Goddess lived, so her memory lingers more strongly here. Also, the closer one draws to the Imperial City, the more danger there is. Even today, after a thousand years, those who rule feel threatened by the power of the Goddess."

"Come," said the man. "It is time to leave. I fear we may have revealed too much."

The little family started down the mountainside. Two days later, when they were making their way down from the foothills, they saw below in the fields what looked like a plume of smoke. When they came closer, they heard a strange roar.

The next moment, the sky was blotted with a black cloud and they were pelted with hail as hard as ivory balls. Clever-Lazy and her parents could hardly breathe, see, or hear one another cry out in terror.

When they opened their eyes again, they saw that the landscape had been ravaged; every green leaf and blade had been destroyed for miles around. The struggling new grain crop they had rejoiced over a few mornings before was now totally destroyed.

When they reached the village, they ran toward their bakery and the house attached to it. Clever-Lazy rushed first into her bedroom and slid open the screen. Outside her window stood the little almond tree stripped bare of every blossom.

4

Changes

THE DAYS THAT followed were sad and terrible. There was hardly any food to eat, nor any hope, now, of a harvest to come. The rivers overran their banks, flooded the fields and crept into the very houses. The water in the wells turned blood-red and bred sickness. Many people left the village, joining the thousands of others who came through on the roads.

Baker and her husband talked far into the night and decided that they would try to reach the Imperial City, which lay far away in another province. The wife of a distant cousin kept a shop there. She sold bowls and kettles. Long ago, when she wrote that she had been widowed, Clever-Lazy's father had sent her money so she would not have to lose her husband's business. Perhaps she would be able to give them shelter while they looked for new work.

But when the morning came, and time to start the journey, Baker's husband did not waken from his sleep. He had

died in the night, partly of the water sickness and partly
from lack of food. Clever-Lazy and her mother discovered
that during the last week of his life, he had not eaten his
portion of the bread they shared, but had put it aside in
a basket, which he had hidden in the great cold oven. He
had also left them money to pay the river captain, and a
note telling them of his love and hopes for them. He asked
them to use the bread and the money on their journey to
the house of his cousin's wife in the distant city.

Just as they left their house, Baker paused at the doorway and said, "Look about quickly, Clever-Lazy, and take
the one thing you value most. Make sure that it is easily
carried."

Tears came into Clever-Lazy's eyes. She did not hesitate.
She flung open a chest, and her hand sought the familiar
curve of the handle on the red lacquered box that her father
and mother had made for her story figures. She rejoined her
mother on the doorstep. They did not bother to lock the
house or shop. "I would rather whosoever enters does so as
my guest," said Baker.

They set off on the road that led toward the river. On
the way, the fever and sickness that had stricken her father
now fell upon Clever-Lazy and her mother. Somehow,
despite her own sickness, Baker managed to get the two of
them to the river; somehow she found and paid for a place
on the deck of the riverboat. How many days they sailed
on the Great River, Clever-Lazy never knew. She was barely
aware of her mother's presence and, once in a while, of
green hills sliding by. Once she thought she heard her

mother's voice raised in anger and the sounds of a scuffle, but she was too weak to be concerned and lapsed into her fevered dream again.

When she awoke, after several days, she found her mother's anxious face bending over her. At last Clever-Lazy fell into a restful sleep, unmarred this time by fever. When she awoke again, she found her mother sicker than she. Other passengers had stolen their bread and their money. All that was left was a little box of dried herbs and the box of story figures, made of good flour, sugar, eggs and corn starch. The story soldiers, eaten one by one, had saved Clever-Lazy's life.

That night, her mother, Baker, descendant of ancient priestesses, died in her sleep. She, like so many others who failed to complete the journey, was slipped over the side of the boat into the arms of the Great River.

Two days later, the riverboat arrived at its destination. Clever-Lazy had found her father's cousin's address stuck in the lining of the box. She knew the cousin's name-sign was the same as her own, and that the cousin lived in rooms behind the Shop of the Blue Door in the Street of Kettles. She assumed that all she would have to do was ask up and down the streets of the city, much as a stranger would have asked the way in her own village.

When she disembarked from the riverboat, she gazed about the wharf and was amazed by the swarm of people who rushed about, each intent on his or her own purpose. Finding her father's cousin's wife would be more difficult than she had thought! Red box in one hand, a bundle of clothes in the other, she lingered at the waterfront before plunging into the maze of streets that led away from the river. The sun shone in a blue sky, a crisp breeze crinkled the current, and a family of ducks swam in and out of the shadows of ships and pilings. When a caravan of camels came stalking along the quay, she backed away, gaping in astonishment. The world was full of many marvels! Despite her grief for her mother, Clever-Lazy felt happiness and excitement well up inside of her. Gratefully, she sent up a prayer of thanks to the Goddess.

Elephants she had seen before. She watched while half a dozen of them lifted great teak logs to the deck of a waiting vessel. Nearby another vessel was being unloaded. She observed carefully as workers hauled boxes and bales from the ship's hold, the men timing their actions to the rhythm of their chants. The fiber rope slung over a boom made the crudest kind of pulley. Already she could think of ways to improve it. She sought out the foreman and tried to talk with him. There was so much noise, and he seemed so angry that she gave up shouting back at him and retreated further down the wharf.

From the deck of the ship, two gangplanks extended. A line of women swayed beneath the weight of baskets of grain on their heads. They never broke the rhythm of their walk. Once on deck, each tipped her basket's contents into the hold, then returned down the second plank for still another load. Naked to the waist, they wore skirts knotted over their hips, which fell just short of their ankles. Sweat glistened on their bodies and on their muscular arms. Not one of them returned Clever-Lazy's smile.

"Gawker! Bumpkin!" a rough voice growled in her ear. The words were almost lost in the clatter of horses' hooves and the rattle of a swiftly-drawn carriage that was now rolling over the very spot where Clever-Lazy had been standing. Whoever had pushed her out of harm's way had hurried on, too busy to be thanked or complained to. Wet and bruised, Clever-Lazy picked herself up from the puddle she had fallen into and limped off the wharf.

All day she wandered up and down the streets of the Imperial City, marveling at signs and banners, stalls and shops, crafts and trades, and most overwhelming of all, people. There seemed to be people of every age and size and color and costume and temper. If she paused to watch or wonder, there was always somebody to push her on to new sights and sounds and smells. At length she became quite bewildered and was not at all certain in which direction the river lay, whether she had walked along certain streets before or was going in circles. Several times she asked people for directions to the Street of Kettles, but they were either too busy to answer, said they didn't know, or gave instructions based on landmarks she could not recognize.

When evening came, the pace of the city barely seemed to slacken, but the smell of thousands of suppers was wafted on the warm air. Clever-Lazy realized she was hungry and crept into a doorway to open her box. She had eaten most of the lesser characters while still on the river voyage. She felt tears prickle as she thought of the kindness and understanding her mother had shown in leaving her favorite characters to the last. One by one, she took the figures out of the box and laid them on the doorstep in front of her.

'Perhaps,' she thought, 'if I eat the Proud Maiden, I shall become more brave and adventurous. And if I eat the dragon, I shall partake of strength and fierceness. And if I eat the Emperor and Empress, I shall become wise and good.'

She looked up to find that a small circle of children had gathered around her, watching her. Almost before she knew it, she had launched into a variation of the tale she had told long ago to her parents and the wandering tinker. By the time she was finished, a few adults had joined the little audience. Someone threw a copper coin into the lid of her box, and a few more rattled in beside it. The mother of one of the children offered her a rice cake, and another gave her a dollop of meat sauce wrapped in a cabbage leaf.

When her listeners had left, Clever-Lazy carefully fitted her story figures back into their places. "Well, at any rate, I shan't eat you tonight," she whispered to Proud Maiden as she closed the box. Then, creeping into a wicker cask that stood in the dark corner of the doorway, she arranged her bundle of clothes as a pillow, gathered the box as close to her as possible, curled herself into a ball and fell asleep.

For the next few weeks, Clever-Lazy lived by her wits. Mostly, with the aid of the painted dough figures, she told stories she already knew and invented others. Once she was paid to mind a child for a few hours. Another time she fixed a toy and, having shown her skill at that task, was asked to do some sewing. Alas, Clever-Lazy had never learned to sew. But she could write; she wrote letters for hire. She was never paid much, but she managed to keep herself fed, and at night, she always found herself a doorway or an alley to sleep in. Certainly she was thinner, and I am afraid she was nowhere nearly as well-scrubbed and tidy as her mother would have wished. Indeed, you might not have recognized her.

It was only by chance that Tinker rediscovered Clever-Lazy. He was jogging along the street, the tools of his trade on his back and a bamboo pole balanced across his shoulders. Strings of bowls and kettles hung from the pole. His wares made a gentle clash as he trotted along, and his thoughts were, as usual, practical ones, mostly about the price of copper. Suddenly, he found it necessary to swerve in order to avoid a little knot of people who were gathered around a street entertainer.

Tinker's main concern was to avoid crashing his long pole into someone. Afterward, he remembered being annoyed because a copper can was almost knocked off by a member of the crowd too entranced to notice him. In stopping to rescue it, he became aware that the crowd was listening to a story. Something in the tone of voice made him strain to stand on tiptoe to catch a glimpse of the storyteller.

Next moment, never minding squawks and grumbles from the gaping listeners, he shouldered his way, pole and all, to the front of the crowd and found himself staring into the face of a thin and ragged little creature with unkempt hair and an unbelievably dirty face. She stared back at him; then Clever-Lazy's voice cried out, "Why, it's Tinker! Our own dear Tinker!" as she flung her arms around his neck.

5

In the Tea House

AS SOON AS they could get away from the crowd, Tinker and Clever-Lazy found a tea house where they could talk. Tinker ordered tea and dumplings for himself, a whole meal for Clever-Lazy. He watched with pleasure as she attacked the several bowls of food set in front of her, and was disappointed when she leaned back and confessed that she could not eat as much as in the old days. Months of small portions or no food at all had pinched her appetite. However, she was more than happy to sit and talk over a pot of tea.

Tinker, who had been fond of her parents and touched by their kindness to him, listened with tears in his eyes to Clever-Lazy's description of their last days. Clever-Lazy then told him, with some pride, about her adventures and enterprises since she had arrived in the city. Tinker was neither admiring nor amused.

"I must take you to your cousin-in-law at once," he said. "I know the Street of Kettles and the Shop of the Blue Door quite well. Often I have business there. I never dreamed the owner could be related to your father although her name-sign is the same. Your father was always so gentle and generous and understanding, while she is not."

"Not? Tinker, what do you mean?"

"Not as gentle, generous and understanding. But no one could be that," said Tinker. "Your parents were unique, Clever-Lazy. I am honored to have known them and to have been their guest. Now I am honored to aid their daughter and to escort her to the home of her relatives. It is the least I can do."

"Perhaps I don't want to go to my relatives," said Clever-Lazy. "I am doing quite well on my own. How old were you, Tinker, when you first set out in the world?"

"Too young," Tinker sighed. "My father died before I was born, killed by bandits on the road. My mother died at my birthing. My father's father brought me up and taught me our family trade. He was a good coppersmith, and taught me to mend bowls and kettles and understand the nature of metals. Just as important, he taught me to live on the road and that's a craft in itself. A good tinker who mends honestly soon works himself out of a job in any one neighborhood, and has to move to another. My grand-father, and perhaps his grandfather, had a regular route that he followed, which went as far as the Province of Dancing Mountains, then back by river to the city again. My grandfather was too old to travel by the time I was born, but he drew maps and he made me study them, and he pushed me out onto the road when I was no more than a child. He taught me to fend and cope and follow my nose. Most important, he taught me to sense danger and to avoid evil."

"Well, if you managed to survive, so can I," said Clever-Lazy.

Tinker shook his head, disagreeing. "My grandfather always warned me and I know for myself he spoke the truth: the dangers of city streets are worse than those of a lonely road. In the winters, when we stayed in the city, I learned to be streetwise. I learned that kind of wiseness – it is not really wisdom – when I was just a little boy. But you were born in a remote village, Clever-Lazy, with kind and loving parents to look after you. Your parents would never forgive me if I leave you to the streets."

"But my parents are not here," said Clever-Lazy. "They might change their minds entirely if they saw how clever I am at earning my own way."

"I don't believe that," rejoined the tinker. "You don't understand the dangers here. There are evil and wicked people in the world, Clever-Lazy, who could do you great harm."

"I agree that evil exists," Clever-Lazy said. "My parents used to say, 'Recognize a demon and call him by his name,' and 'Meet a dragon on the road, draw your sword in awareness.' I am not stupid, Tinker. Nor am I ignorant. I've seen and learned much since I left our village."

"That's just what worries me," said Tinker. "I don't think a girl should know so much. I don't want you to know about evil."

"What do you mean by that?" asked Clever-Lazy, anger edging her voice. "Are you trying to tell me that I should not be responsible for knowing the difference between good and evil? Do you mean to sit there and drink tea and tell me that you should pick and choose what I should see and learn?" Two red spots had appeared in Clever-Lazy's cheeks. "I don't think the Goddess would care much for that!"

"Goddess?" asked Tinker, bewildered. A little while ago he had ordered a quiet cup of tea; now he felt that he was floundering in hot water.

"She is the guardian of our family. She is the one who hears our prayers. Before the Great Calamity, she —"

Tinker, scandalized, interrupted. He lowered his voice. "Never speak of this goddess again. You could have us arrested. I don't know where you get such disgraceful ideas."

Tears sprang to Clever-Lazy's eyes. She fought them back into her throat, but her voice cracked with the effort. "Oh, Tinker! I was so happy when I first saw you. How is it that you make me so sad and angry? I thought you were my friend."

Tinker lived such a lonely life that he was not used to emotion. He glanced around the tea house uncomfortably. "Shhh!" he hissed. "Someone may hear you." A waitress came over to their table to clear the plates and bring a new pot of tea. The water in the earthen pot was so hot that it welled up through the short, straight spout and made a little puddle on the table.

Clever-Lazy was reminded of her own hot tears welling up. She tried to pretend, until the waitress was gone, that she was elaborately interested in a vase of lilies. She took a flower from the vase. "There is something wrong with the design of this spout. It should be shaped like this lily. See how I twist the neck down and up again? The dip could be a steam trap that will keep the steam from spitting out and burning a person or making a puddle . . ."

She stopped because the tinker had reached across the table and was squeezing her arm.

"Clever-Lazy," said Tinker, "sometimes I could twist *your* neck!"

"And why should you want to do that?"

"Because I am so concerned about you."

"A fine way to show it," she scoffed, indicating her arm. Then she giggled. She had no way of knowing, of course, but she sounded very like her mother when her mother was young and giggly.

Tinker flushed, then let go of her arm hastily. But he continued with what he had to say: "How do you manage to drag teapots and lilies into a conversation when I am talking about something serious and important? Listen to what I am saying, Clever-Lazy! You must find some way to be looked after, and if you won't make the effort, then I must do it for you."

At that, Clever-Lazy stopped giggling. "Listen yourself, Tinker. I am an inventor. Not only do I invent things, but I invent ways to make my own living. People pay me to tell stories. I have half a bag of coppers to prove it. Soon I will have enough money to make a whole new cast of characters out of dough, and then I shall invent *new* stories."

"Where will you tell your stories when winter comes?" asked Tinker. "Ahah! I suppose you have never given a thought to winter."

"I've given it much thought," replied Clever-Lazy coolly. "I invent other things besides stories, Tinker. I advised the kite maker how to make a better kite. One day, I think I could design one big enough for a person to glide around on. Oh, but that can wait," she said, sensing the tinker's disbelief and rising impatience. "I know everything there is to know about the baking business. I plan to call on all the bakers in the city and offer to tell them how to run their businesses. I have a thousand and one ideas and I have a new one every minute."

"Ah so!" said Tinker, barely concealing his triumph as he thought he had won the argument. His voice became heavy with irony. "I have noticed, Clever-Lazy, that most people, Clever-Lazy, do not appreciate being told how to run their own business, my dear Clever-Lazy. Especially by a mere girl, Clever-Lazy." He saw that Clever-Lazy was about to interrupt, and waved his hands to silence her. Then he half rose from his chair, leaned across the table and waggled a finger under her nose. For a young man, who a short while before had been wary of any show of emotion in public, he was behaving in a most extraordinary fashion.

"Oh, you have ideas aplenty, Clever-Lazy, but you have no practical experience. Why, I happen to know you never even helped with the dishes!"

If he thought that Clever-Lazy would be crushed by his remarks, he was wrong. "Anyone can learn to wash dishes," replied Clever-Lazy haughtily. "But how many can invent a better teapot — or kettle? I could sell you the design for a new kettle, Tinker, that might not be improved upon for a thousand years. Why, I could make your fortune!"

Tinker chose to ignore this last remark. He poured another cup of tea for Clever-Lazy and himself and sat steeped in thought, watching the tea grounds settle to the bottom of his cup. Then he sighed and spoke again, not as excitedly but with serious concern.

"Earning a living is not the only thing I'm talking about," he said. "There are people who will not give a fig for your inventions. They'd see only that you are a woman, a mere girl, alone and unprotected. Sooner or later, someone would seize upon you, twist your goodness to their own evil purpose. You would be lost, Clever-Lazy. Lost to yourself! That, I cannot bear to think about. I will not bear witness, nor will I turn my back and go away. I care too much for your parents' memory to do that."

"But I know that women live here in the city and live by themselves," Clever-Lazy argued. "My own father's cousin's wife manages alone."

"Yes, but she has a shop. She is a woman of property. And, besides, she is a widow. A respectable widow is not regarded in the same way as a girl who lives on the streets."

"I know a woman who is a moneylender. She is very old and powerful."

"But she is old."

"Now I know what you are talking about!" exclaimed Clever-Lazy. "I have seen girls who are no older than I who stand in doorways and lean out of windows to talk to passersby. When I try to talk to them, they will have nothing to do with me. They chatter much about nothing and paint their faces with vermillion and kohl, and whiten their complexions with rice flour. They live in the House of Flowers and sell their favors to men."

Tinker sputtered and put down his tea. "How come you to know about such things?"

"My mother told me," said Clever-Lazy. "She said I should pity such and remember they are women, too, and therefore loved by the Goddess. But I know that happiness does not lie in that direction."

"I am glad to know you know," said the tinker, feeling a little dazed.

"So you see, my dear Tinker, I am not stupid; neither am I ignorant. I can make a life for myself just as you can. This may be a wicked city, but there is goodness, too. In these few weeks, I have learned to thread my way through streets and alleyways; so, too, I can learn to pick my way between good and evil."

"Remember, for all your cleverness, Clever-Lazy, you have not yet found the Street of Kettles. I strongly suspect that you have not really tried. That proves that you are not yet ready to be trusted on your own. So far you have gotten by on luck and the fact that you are so scrawny and scruffy that no one would want you anyway."

"No one?" asked Clever-Lazy.

"No one," repeated Tinker, firmly.

Clever-Lazy sighed. "I just thought," she said carelessly, "that I might ask a tinker to go into partnership with me. I could invent, and he could carry out my designs."

"Not *this* tinker," returned Tinker decidedly. He was surprised to feel his heart give a little lurch. He hoped his voice did not betray him. "To be a tinker's wife is no life for a woman. My mother died young and so did my grandmother. I do not intend to marry — ever."

"Who said anything about marriage?" asked Clever-Lazy. "I was only thinking of a partnership, a business partnership. In time, we could own a workshop together and share the profits."

"That proves it, Clever-Lazy," he said. "I must take you to your cousin's shop right away, and put you in the hands of a respectable woman." A look of dismay crossed Clever-Lazy's face. He relented a little and quickly added, "Oh, I shall come to visit you from time to time to see if you have learned any common sense. That much I owe to your parents."

"And to me?" asked Clever-Lazy. "My parents are dead. I am here *now*. What do you owe me?"

Tinker frowned as though assessing a debt. Then his face cleared. A new idea shone out. "I owe you nothing, Clever-Lazy." He laughed out loud at her indignation. "I will come to see you because I *want* to!"

But in the end, this was not what persuaded Clever-Lazy to give in. Her parents had wanted her to reach her father's cousin's house so much that they were willing to die to that end. To halfheartedly search for her relative and not be able to find her was quite different from having Tinker appear and offer to direct her.

Perhaps, she told herself, the Goddess had sent him.

6

Behind the Blue Door

SHOPSHREWD HAD BEEN expecting for months that her dead husband's relatives would arrive from the Province of Dancing Mountains. The rooms behind the shop were small and cramped, and she was hard put to find space for herself and her children. Her husband's relative had assured her by letter that he, his wife and daughter would stay only a short time, but Shopshrewd was skeptical of such a promise. She knew that if she had lent money to a distant relative, she would have sought to squeeze out every drop in return.

Shopshrewd had three children. Little Prune, a quiet, anxious little girl about nine years old, was a worrier and a tattletale. She would have liked to smooth out every eruption of joy or anger or sorrow, either in herself or others. She preferred her world to be flat. The effort to keep it so cost her a puckered brow and a strange sort of breathlessness. Often she held her breath.

Prickle, who was about seven, delighted in getting Little Prune into trouble. The best way to do that was to tease P'loy, the baby of the family. P'loy was not really a baby. He was five years old and big and strong for his age, but his mother could not bear for him to grow up. She had carried him about as long as she could, fed him on special foods and presented him with little gifts and special privileges denied to the other children.

Little Prune's life was made miserable by fear of P'loy's howls and screams, which would summon her mother from the shop. She tried to get even, or keep ahead of Prickle, by running to her mother and putting even his innocent activities in the worst possible light. Shopshrewd complained that Prickle's badness was some mysterious inheritance from his father's family. Had not his father the thoughtlessness to die young and leave her to care for the shop and three children? And now the wretched man's relatives were about to arrive.

When weeks went by and no one came, Shopshrewd half hoped that the baker's husband and his family had perished in the floods and famine known to be sweeping the countryside. But when Tinker appeared with Clever-Lazy in tow, she decided that there might be some advantage in accepting the girl. She soon let her neighbors and her customers know that if it were not for her, Clever-Lazy would have starved or come to shame on the streets. But, best of all, Clever-Lazy was only one more mouth to feed. She could earn her keep by sweeping the shop, scrubbing the floors, marketing and cooking and minding the children. Alas for Shopshrewd. She did not know our Clever-Lazy.

Clever-Lazy had no intention of being slow, clumsy, inept, irresponsible, destructive, obstructive, corruptive or stupid, yet within a week Shopshrewd made her feel, and she made herself feel, that she was all of these. She had rarely thought about how the ordinary work of a household was done. When she was asked to sweep the shop, she was surprised not so much that it was a dull and awkward job, but that it took a kind of skill to do it quickly and effectively. Even more surprising, it had to be done several times a day, every day.

So, here stands Clever-Lazy, broom in hand. She tried holding the broom in new and different ways. She tried cutting the bushy end of the broom into new shapes and angles. She tried shortening the bamboo handle. This made her look more closely at the hollowness of the handle and decide that the broom should not have any bristles at all. Instead, she told herself, it should be constructed as an open tube through which the dust could be sucked into a bag or jar by some sort of giant's breath.

She was so engrossed that she did not notice that P'loy had sat down among the bristles and was playing with them. Prickle scooped up a handful and dumped them down the neck of P'loy's jacket, causing him to bellow. Little Prune tried to reach a hand up under the quilted jacket, which, I must confess, was already stretched to bursting point over a broad back.

When Shopshrewd came to see what all the screaming was about, she found the floor unswept and Clever-Lazy sitting in the middle of a worse mess than she had started with. All about her were strewn bits of bristle and lengths of broom handle. And there sat Clever-Lazy with her cheeks puffing in and out while she made strange noises through a sawed-off piece of bamboo. How was Shopshrewd to know that Clever-Lazy was in the midst of inventing the vacuum cleaner? Afterward, she told her neighbor, Ever Curious, "I really think the girl is crazy," but at the moment, she flew at Clever-Lazy and began to hit her with the other end of the sawed-off broom.

Since Clever-Lazy was a baker's daughter, Shopshrewd assumed that she would know how to cook and bake. Clever-Lazy had been encouraged to observe and take notes about what went on in the kitchen, and to experiment with extraordinary concoctions, but she had never done the daily cooking.

When Shopshrewd asked her to cook the evening rice, she remembered that her mother had cooked the rice in boiling water. She filled a medium-sized pot with water and set it on the stove. She was hungry and decided she could probably eat two bowlsful at least. She assumed that Shopshrewd and each of the three children could do the same. She already knew P'loy well enough to guess that he would eat as much or more than the rest of them.

Carefully, Clever-Lazy measured out ten bowls of rice and poured the amount into boiling water. Always observant, she noticed that the water stopped boiling and that the pile of rice sat sullenly in the bottom of the pot. Nothing happened. Clever-Lazy added more fuel to the fire. The pot started bubbling again. The bubbles turned thick and milky. White streaks of starch ran down the sides of the pot. Clever-Lazy grabbed a wet rag to clean the pot. As the moisture in the cloth turned instantly to steam, it burned her hand.

The mound of rice grew alarmingly. Each grain of rice soaked up water, puffed itself to two or three times its former size. Soon there was more rice than water in the pot. Like some terrible white genie, the rice began to rise higher than the rim and to run down the sides, following the streaks already left by the bubbles. Despite her sore hand, Clever-Lazy grabbed a pot lid and tried to cram rice and steam back into the pot. The rice fought back at her. The rice kept coming. Now it was creeping across the brazier, dropping to the floor!

When Shopshrewd, summoned by Little Prune, came into the kitchen, she discovered Clever-Lazy running frantically about in search of more and more bowls into which to ladle the huge expanding mound. Rice, in various and sundry containers, was set about on tables, shelves and even the floor. P'loy was sitting on the tabletop, picking up handsful of rice and cramming them into his mouth. Prickle was laughing excitedly, dancing about the room showering himself with handsful of rice. Clever-Lazy began to giggle, too.

Clever-Lazy's parents would have laughed with her and praised her good intentions while they soothed the burned hand. They would have encouraged her to sort out her thoughts, and write notes about what she had observed. But Shopshrewd was not like her parents.

She yelled and screamed and complained that fate had forced her to harbor a stupid girl who wasted the very food that was provided for her and burned her hand on purpose so that she could not clean up the mess.

Poor Clever-Lazy! She was truly sorry. She knew that Shopshrewd worked hard to provide for her and the children. She just wished that she would not tell them so often. Her parents had worked hard too, yet they made her feel clever and loved. For the first time in her life, she felt guilty and worthless.

The Goddess seemed very far away.

Almost two months passed before Tinker came to the Imperial City again. All the time he trudged the roads, he had been thinking of Clever-Lazy. Although his mind told him that what he had done was right, his heart whispered otherwise. As soon as he reached the city, he rushed to the Shop of the Blue Door and asked for Clever-Lazy. She was cleaner and plumper than when he last saw her, but he could not help noticing that much of the brightness had gone out of her eyes. He contrived to be alone with her for a few minutes. "Is Shopshrewd ever cruel to you?" he asked.

"Not really," returned Clever-Lazy. "She hits me sometimes when I have done something stupid, but she does not actually beat me. She sees that I have enough to eat and she has found some of her old clothes for me. She's kind enough in her own way."

Tinker was baffled by her meekness, disturbed by the deadness of her voice. He longed to shake her, to shout at her, to put loving arms about her. Instead he turned the conversation to other matters. "I have been thinking much about teapots," he said brusquely, "and the shape of their spouts. Perhaps you forget, but we talked about such matters at the tea house."

Clever-Lazy gave a sad little smile. "I had almost forgotten," she said. "I remember now that we did talk about teapots. You were quite annoyed with me, in fact." For a moment, the old Clever-Lazy flickered. "I made myself think about teapots as a sort of trick to keep back my tears."

"Maybe the trick will work again," said Tinker, and was rewarded by a tremulous smile. "Now here's my drawing, Clever-Lazy. I'm not sure I have the curve quite right . . ."

Clever-Lazy bent over the drawing, interested in spite of herself. "You are right, Tinker. I mean that you are right that you are wrong. The curve should bulge more at the bottom. There should be a steam trap at the base so that the steam can expand. It will hover at the opening to keep the tea in the teapot hot until it's ready to pour." Clever-Lazy had seized a piece of charcoal and was making drawings as she talked. She thrust out her hand to show Tinker a place where new pink skin covered a recent burn. "I've been thinking about steam lately," she said, and told the story of the rice. They laughed so hard that Shopshrewd came in and told Tinker he should be off.

Before he finished packing his wares, Tinker was able to seize a few more words with Clever-Lazy. "I understand the reason for the bulge much better now, but I am still not certain how to translate your drawing into hammered copper. See if you can find a potter who will make us a model in clay, and I shall figure out how best to copy it. Perhaps you will make us rich, Clever-Lazy."

When Clever-Lazy smiled at him, Tinker's heart gave a little leap.

7

Making Money

SHOPSHREWD SOLD NOT only metal vessels, but clay pots and bowls as well. The next time she ran short of cheap rice bowls, Clever-Lazy volunteered to run to the nearby potter's yard. Before starting off, she rolled up her sketches of the teapot and thrust them into her sleeve. After she had delivered Shopshrewd's order, she took out the drawings and asked the potter if he would make a pot according to her design. He did not want to be bothered. Besides, he said, he had always made pots with short, straight spouts and so had his father before him.

Clever-Lazy would have turned away defeated, but fortunately, the potter's wife had been hovering nearby, dipping bowls into vats of glaze. As Clever-Lazy was leaving the yard, Bowlmaker (for that was her name) hurried after her and caught up just outside the gate. She asked to look at the sketches.

"Let *me* try to make such a teapot," she whispered hoarsely. Then, interpreting the amazement on Clever-Lazy's face as doubt, she rushed to plead her case: "Yes, I am a potter, too. My family have always been potters, not only my father but my mother and my grandmother. My old granny used to say that our honorable ancestors would have starved to death if they had had to rely on what was brought home from the hunt. Women supplied most of the food by gathering and gleaning. It was they who invented jars and pots to store seed and carry water."

"You sound like my mother," said Clever-Lazy.

"And a good and sensible woman she must be," returned Bowlmaker. She reached for the drawings. "Look for me when I come with the rice bowls. I'll bring some clay with me, and we can work together on your design."

A few days later, Bowlmaker came into the shop to deliver the rice bowls. She had seen Shopshrewd and the children go by the potter's yard on the way to the bazaar (they were going to buy P'loy a new quilted jacket) and had seized the opportunity to hurry round to the Blue Door. She had brought a model in unfired clay that was still soft enough for Clever-Lazy to pinch and smooth into new shapes. Clever-Lazy was able to show her how the spout should dip a little more at the base. On her part, Bowlmaker persuaded Clever-Lazy that the proportions would be more pleasing if the spout rose a little higher at the end. "Even if people don't understand the reason for the change, Clever-Lazy, I think they will buy the new design because it is graceful and satisfying to the eye. Later, they will notice the advantages of owning a teapot that pours without sputtering, and keeps the water hot for a longer time."

Bowlmaker was anxious to keep the project secret and advised Clever-Lazy to do the same. "I am tired of working as a master potter all these long years for no money, Clever-Lazy. I have been looking for a venture such as this that would be entirely my own. Now *I* can pocket some money."

Between them, Bowlmaker and Clever-Lazy agreed that they would sell the new teapot exclusively to the Shop of the Blue Door, provided that Shopshrewd would buy all that they made. Shopshrewd would profit from the markup she would add after paying Bowlmaker. Since she would have an "exclusive," no one could buy one of the better-designed teapots except from her. No doubt she would charge more than she did for an ordinary teapot. Bowlmaker, unbeknownst to Shopshrewd, would then pay Clever-Lazy two coins out of every twelve she received for making the pot. She would keep the rest for herself to pay for the cost of clay, the molding and firing, and allow a profit for herself.

"You are being paid for your brains," said Bowlmaker ticking off on her fingers, "I am being paid for my skills, and 'Shrewd is being paid for her ability to run a shop."

Only then did Clever-Lazy tell her how Tinker planned to produce the same design in copper once a model had been made in clay. Bowlmaker scowled, thinking, then allowed her brow to smooth. "All right," she said, "I'll agree to that. His copper kettle will boil water over flame; my teapot will be used to hold the water after it has boiled. We won't be in competition and people will have to buy both, kettle and pot."

She paused and raised her eyebrows. "Ahah and o-hoh!" she chortled. Clever-Lazy unaccountably blushed. "I think you are rather fond of this Tinker person. My fantasy was that he was an old man, but now I am beginning to wonder if he is young and handsome?"

"We are old friends, nothing more," Clever-Lazy hastened to explain. "Tinker knew me long ago when I lived with my parents in the Province of Dancing Mountains." She made her voice as dignified as possible. "We speak mainly of pots and kettles."

"So you are from the Province of Dancing Mountains," said Bowlmaker. "You are a long way from your birthplace." She hesitated. "They say that the women there are different from all others. And there *is* something different about you, Clever-Lazy. I knew it the moment you walked into the yard."

"Perhaps it is because some of us still believe in the —" began Clever-Lazy. Before she could finish, Bowlmaker clapped a hand over her mouth.

"I do not want to know what you believe," she said. Then, releasing the startled Clever-Lazy, she whispered in a harsh voice, "My old granny warned me against such as you, Clever-Lazy. 'There is too much danger,' she said, 'in believing in old beliefs.' Yet, as she lay dying, she spoke about . . . Well, no matter! I like you, Clever-Lazy, but keep your dangerous thoughts to yourself."

When next Tinker came to see Clever-Lazy, he noticed
right away that she looked happier. She showed him the
teapot, which was already being sold at the Shop of the
Blue Door, and told him of the secret financial arrangement she had made with Bowlmaker. To her surprise, he
pursed his lips in disapproval, and told her that he didn't
like the idea of her being paid behind Shopshrewd's back.

"But she will take all my money away from me," wailed
Clever-Lazy. "I like making money. I want to feel inde-
pendent."

"You can't *steal* independence," argued Tinker. "Shopshrewd makes herself a prisoner. She's so afraid someone
will cheat her, she can't allow herself to enjoy life."

"But that's what I'm telling you!" Clever-Lazy retorted,
feeling herself go hot. "She's mean and stingy!"

"Then so are you," said Tinker. "If you don't tell her
that you are making money through her shop, you are
not much different. Shopshrewd provides you with food
and clothes and a roof over your head. What do you do in
return?"

Clever-Lazy hung her head. A slow, dull blush burned in
her cheeks. "I've learned to sweep and to cook rice. I'm
much more useful than I used to be."

"But don't you see? I don't want her to look upon you as
merely useful. You are more than that, Clever-Lazy. Stop
acting like a serving girl who is forever cheating her mistress. Let Shopshrewd know you are clever and efficient in
your own way. Let her know that you are making money
from that teapot and offer to pay your keep."

"But *I'm* afraid to speak. She'll be angry with me."

"She's angry now for no particular reason."

"I resent her more than ever lately."

"Take a risk, Clever-Lazy. Decide what you want from her, then ask for it."

"Oh, Tinker!" exploded Clever-Lazy. "I look forward to your coming for weeks and weeks, then when you come, we do nothing but argue. You are supposed to be my best friend, yet you make life so difficult for me."

Tinker sighed. "It's the same with me, Clever-Lazy. When I'm on the road, I store up all the things I'm going to share with you. I heard a bird sing by moonlight. I saw a gnarled old man planting gnarled brown taro roots. I saw a string of purple eggplants being carried to market. Because of you, I see so much more and I *am* so much more, Clever-Lazy. But now you're so angry, there's no use to share."

Tears pricked under her eyelids as she watched him pack his wares. She turned her back on him. Not until he was gone could she make sure that he had taken one of the new teapots with him. She went into the back of the shop to prepare the evening meal. She clattered pots and pans and muttered to herself as she chopped the vegetables. She said hardly a word all during the meal, but after she had scrubbed the cooking space and put the children to bed, she sought out Shopshrewd who was doing her accounts. "I want to talk to you," she said.

Two months later when Tinker returned, he was able to announce, "I have something to show you." He drew a quilted bag out of his pack from which he produced not the clay pot, but a shiny copper kettle copied almost line for line, but constructed on a larger scale. "I lived with that teapot until I saw it in my sleep," he said. "Then I carved a wooden mold, slightly bigger, and pressed a thin sheet of copper over the shape. I hammered and hammered until I got what I wanted."

"Oh, it's beautiful!" exclaimed Clever-Lazy. "However did you manage the spout?"

"Base and spout are separate pieces, of course. They had to be soldered on with tin."

"Where's the teapot so I can compare?" asked Clever-Lazy.

"I no longer have it," explained Tinker. "Everyone who saw it wanted to buy. I finally sold it at double its price to a wealthy landlord who would not take no for an answer. I still have the mold of course, and I have more orders than I'll be able to carry, both for teapots and kettles."

"Business has been good here, too," said Clever-Lazy. "People we've never seen before come into the shop to ask for 'the kettle that doesn't spill.' Bowlmaker is making lots of money, and so is Shopshrewd." She hesitated. "I am faring well, too. And now I pay for my room and board."

Tinker's face was reddened by sun and wind, but he reddened a shade deeper. "I . . . I want to apologize, Clever-Lazy. I cannot imagine what made me be so rude to you last time. I have no right to tell you what you should or shouldn't do."

Clever-Lazy blushed, too. "You always expect so much of me, in such unexpected ways, Tinker. You were right when you told me to take a risk. Shopshrewd doesn't take my money. I *pay* her."

"Does she treat you any better?"

"I treat myself better. When you said I was as stingy as she is, you frightened me. I suppose that's why I was so angry with you."

"I was afraid you'd *still* be angry with me. What changed your mind?"

Clever-Lazy giggled. "I saw a basket of eggplants being taken to market. They looked like jewels." Tinker reached out and took Clever-Lazy's hand, but dropped it hastily.

When Shopshrewd bustled in from the shop, Tinker and Clever-Lazy were sitting at the kitchen table, the kettle between them. Her eyes lit up in speculation. "How much?" she asked, indicating the kettle.

Tinker named a price, a stiff one. "I shall pay Clever-Lazy two-twelfths for the design," he said. "I shall pay her directly, just as Bowlmaker does."

"Besides that, he will be ordering teapots from you to take on the road," interrupted Clever-Lazy. Tinker had opened his mouth as though to speak, but she kicked him, gently, under the table.

"Why should he order from me instead of from Bowlmaker?" asked Shopshrewd.

"Because you have an 'exclusive' with her. You have promised to take all of her new design pots, and she has promised to sell only to you. Now Tinker and I shall buy from you. We will buy so many that we expect a lower price, of course. But you will still make money."

"Pfff! How many teapots can one tinker carry? Hardly worth my trouble, much less a lower price."

"But there are other tinkers!" Clever-Lazy's eyes were bright. "We can have tinkers going into every province. After they have shown samples of our wares, they can take orders, have crates of teapots shipped to certain points along the rivers."

Here Tinker interrupted. "Each tinker has his own territory. They can sell my kettles, too."

Shopshrewd shook her head. "Who's going to do all the work? Who is going to keep track of all this? I know how to run my shop; they do not call me Shopshrewd for nothing, but I don't like the smell of this. It's too big. No, I want nothing to do with it!"

Clever-Lazy and Tinker glanced at each other, baffled. This time it was the tinker who signaled with a fierce look at Clever-Lazy that it was his time to talk. "We all know, Shopshrewd, how clever you are at running your shop."

"And me a poor widow," Shopshrewd reminded him.

"And you a poor widow. But you forget that you have Clever-Lazy working for you now. That puts you at an advantage. Clever-Lazy can write and read and calculate . . ."

"Oh, Shopshrewd, give me a chance! I know I'll make a good manager. I can manage the ordering and the crating and the invoicing. I'll make money for all of us. Soon, just see, the wholesale business will be more important than the shop." She stopped, confused. Tinker had just given her a kick under the table and *his* kick was not gentle.

"Aiee!" wailed Shopshrewd. "So it *is* a plot. The tail would be wagging the dog! Soon you and Tinker will drive me and my children out into the streets. You will laugh up your sleeves while my precious P'loy starves to death." She lunged at Clever-Lazy, the better to slap her across the face, but hit the kettle instead and sent it clattering to the floor.

Tinker persuaded Shopshrewd to sit down at the table while Clever-Lazy made tea. He listened patiently while she complained about the price of copper, the duplicity of salesmen, the stupidity of customers, the scarcity of tin, the difficulties of bringing up children when prices are high and manners low . . . By the time the water had boiled and Clever-Lazy had poured water from the new kettle into one of the new pots, Tinker had managed to calm Shopshrewd enough so that she could drink her tea and discuss the ordinary business that brought him there. Only then did he venture to interest her in a small order of kettles.

"How will you get the kettles to me?" asked Shopshrewd. "I have to be sure of a continued supply, and you are too often on the road."

"I shall be back in two months' time, and then I plan to spend the winter here. I cannot promise to fill your entire order, but I can assure you that if you are willing to pay my price, you will be the sole outlet in the Imperial City."

Clever-Lazy felt her heart flood with joy. "Tinker, do you really mean you will spend the winter here? Perhaps you can rent space in the Street of Kettles? Oh, Tinker, that means I shall see you every day!"

Before Tinker could answer, Shopshrewd was quick to intervene, "Not if I can help it! I'm not about to let a female relative of mine throw herself away on a worthless tinker. Besides, I need you to help in the house and shop. Don't think for a moment that you will be allowed to waste time blabbing to the likes of him!"

Tinker had risen and was standing by the door, his pack on his back. "The day will come when I am as respectable as you are."

Clever-Lazy was puzzled. "But I respect you now," she said. Neither Tinker nor Shopshrewd seemed to hear her.

8

Again the Abacus

SHOPSHREWD DID NOT know what to do with Clever-Lazy. She was afraid of her; at the same time she was disdainful. She consulted with her neighbor, Ever Curious, who agreed that the girl should be watched with suspicion and kept busy. Obviously Clever-Lazy would never become a skilled and enthusiastic housekeeper, but she could read and write. She might as well teach the two boys what might prove useful. As for Little Prune, she was a girl and there was no reason for girls to know too much. Indeed, if one took Clever-Lazy as a model, learning to read and write and figure did more harm than good.

Clever-Lazy tried to remember how it was she had learned. She recalled how much fun she had had with rice starch and bean curd paintings when she was very young and allowed to play about the bakery. Later, she had been given brushes to paint with. When had her pictures become writing? This step had occurred so naturally that it was lost to her, but suddenly she had been able to write her own thoughts and stories, and then to read the written thoughts of others. What she remembered best was her dear parents giving her time to play and make mistakes.

She scrubbed off the kitchen table and put a spoonful of yellow colored starch near one corner of it. She put a spoonful of red starch beside it. Then, rolling up her sleeves, she put one hand in each and began to swirl the colors together. Dreamlike shapes that had no names appeared and disappeared, flowing into one another. When a new color, orange, emerged, the children exclaimed in wonder.

Clever-Lazy looked up and smiled at the children watching her. She spooned out starch onto the other three corners of the table, and indicated that they could play, too. Although she had promised to teach only the two boys how to write, she was determined to include Little Prune too. "Do I have to touch that?" asked Little Prune. "I'll get all messy and Mother will yell at me."

Clever-Lazy hesitated. Little Prune was right. Then Prickle stuck his hand into a mound of red starch and wiped it suddenly across Little Prune's face. P'loy stuck his fingers into the mess, too, and daubed his own broad cheeks. In doing so, he let his tongue steal a taste and, the next moment, he had climbed up onto a bench and bent his face down to the table; the better to lick his share and more. Meanwhile, Prickle chased Little Prune, shrieking, around the room. By the time Shopshrewd rushed into the kitchen, it was a shambles; colored starch was everywhere and P'loy's new quilted jacket was a mottled ruin.

Clever-Lazy changed P'loy into clean clothes, put his jacket to soak in vinegar and banished him to the back room. She replaced pots and pans and dishes, and threw away the broken crockery, glad to know she would be able to use her own money to buy new from Bowlmaker. She swept up spilled rice, poured it back into the sack and enlisted Little Prune and Prickle in the task of picking up beans. In doing so, she remembered how she had learned to sort and count so long ago by playing with the colored beans and beads her parents had given to her.

For a piercing moment, she remembered the little wooden abacus her father had made to her design, and how understanding he had been when she gave it away to the tax collector. He had promised to help her make another, but somehow had never found the time. Her thoughts were interrupted by Little Prune's whine. She had better come into the back room. P'loy had done something she wouldn't like. With a sigh, she put down her broom and followed the bearer of bad news into the room the family used for storing sleeping mats, clothes and their few personal objects.

She pulled back the curtain and saw P'loy sitting on the floor. Crumbs which had dribbled from the corners of his mouth were stuck to his massive chin. Clever-Lazy's red box was open before him. He was holding Proud Maiden in his fat fist. It took another moment to realize he had bitten off her head. He had bitten off the head of every figure in the box. Fleetingly he tried charm; he offered a sickly smile. Something he saw in Clever-Lazy's face caused him to shriek instead.

Clever-Lazy had never been so angry in her entire life. A sheet of fire, pure red rage, swept over her. The next moment, she was rushing toward P'loy, seeing his terror and taking fierce pleasure in it. She grabbed his shoulders, shook him, became aware of her own voice. It was as though it came from another person. P'loy shrieked and turned purple, but no tears accompanied his cries. Tears did spring from Clever-Lazy's eyes, hot, searing tears stored up over weeks and months of loneliness, anger, sadness. They jetted from her eyes, burned her cheeks, ran salty into her mouth.

She became aware of Prickle dancing excitedly on the sidelines. She turned toward him. Unwisely he had placed himself in a corner. She raised her hand, saw him cringe, was glad. She saw Little Prune's frightened face and was suddenly exhausted. Great wracking sobs wrenched out of her chest as she stumbled to her knees and began to pick up pieces of painted dough strewn about the floor. She tried to fit some of them together into a semblance of their old shapes. Then, realizing the uselessness of trying, she put her head down on her arms, sank to the floor and wept.

For the next few days, Clever-Lazy was banished to the front part of the shop while Shopshrewd decided what she would do with her. She was not quite ruthless enough to throw her out on the streets; on the other hand, the girl had brought little but trouble. Except for the teapots. These sold extraordinarily well, and brought new customers into the shop every day. No doubt, when Tinker returned, the kettles would do the same.

As she explained to Ever Curious, she wanted to get rid of Clever-Lazy and she didn't want to get rid of her. Nor did she want to rupture the profitable relationship with Bowlmaker or Tinker, Clever-Lazy's friends. She even thought of marrying her to Tinker, but the two of them together would be a seedbed of schemes. Ever Curious agreed that Clever-Lazy was a problem. Perhaps she might be sold to the House of Flowers, or to a rich gentleman.

Shopshrewd shook her head. She was not a shopkeeper for nothing. Knowing too well Clever-Lazy's talent for trouble, she could foresee the girl's being returned as damaged goods within a week.

Meanwhile Clever-Lazy, listless and dazed, showed the customers what the shop had to offer, figured prices, accepted money. She enjoyed the quiet and being away from the children, but found herself confused by even simple transactions. To help herself, she tucked a handful of beans into the fold of her sleeve and brought them into the shop with her. She arranged them on the countertop in the familiar pattern of thirteen rows of seven beads each. Soon she was engrossed in the pure pleasure of arithmetic working itself out beneath her rapid touch.

A day or two later, when she had set herself some especially difficult calculations, she looked up from the rows of beans and was surprised to discover a customer watching her. He was wearing the embroidered robes of the Emperor's officialdom.

"Where did you learn how to use beans that way, girl?" His tone was so accusing that Clever-Lazy cringed.

"Just playing," she stammered. "Playing with old beans."

The man continued. "That is not mere child's play," he said. "You are using the Emperor's own computing system. Someone must have taught you. What province are you from, girl?"

Shopshrewd, apprehensive at the sound of an urgent male voice, had emerged from behind the curtain at the rear of the shop and stood listening. Now she moved forward to take charge, motioning Clever-Lazy to subside into the background.

"Ah, honored sir," she said, "this is my poor and *distant* relative who is orphaned and left to me to feed and clothe, though I be but a poor widow."

The man made an impatient gesture and turned as though to go out of the shop. Shopshrewd ran from behind the counter, almost put a hand on his arm, thought better of it.

"Oh, sir, I hope this miserable creature has not annoyed or upset you. She is not used to our city ways. Indeed, she may not be quite all right in the head. Now what may I do for you, sir? Honorable sir?"

"You can get out of my way and let me speak to the young woman!"

"Ah, let me speak for her. The poor girl hardly knows or understands. I am sure she is bedazzled out of her wits to be addressed by one such as yourself." A cunning look came into Shopshrewd's eye. "But if, kind sir, you would like to discuss some arrangement with me, her only living relative, we could repair to the rear of the shop. The girl seems stupid and, to less worldly eyes than yours, may not be exactly beautiful. Too plump perhaps? But young girls change. With proper clothes, a little training . . ."

"Woman!" shouted the man. "Stop your blather! I only wish to know from which province the young woman comes, and where she learned to compute with a pattern of thirteen sevens." He pointed (Shopshrewd could hardly believe it) to a handful of beans left on the counter.

"Ah, sir, she is just a country cousin —"

"I come from the Province of Dancing Mountains," interrupted Clever-Lazy.

"Ah, so!" exclaimed the official, seeming to confirm something he had already guessed. "Our Minister of the Imperial Treasure was once a tax collector there, a post that was much lower than mine. Then, out of the blue, he invents a method, a device for computing, that outpaces all the rest of us when we are called before the Emperor. That miserable worm usurped the position for which I was destined —"

"And so richly deserved," murmured Shopshrewd.

"And so richly deserved," agreed the man, giving her a look of grudging respect. "We were each given a computer, a wooden frame inset with beads and rods, and sworn to secrecy. No one but the Emperor's tax collectors are allowed to use the new method. And now this young woman has adapted the secret to a row of beans!"

"I shall discipline her at once," promised Shopshrewd, much frightened. "I shall forbid her to play with beans or count beans or eat beans. I shall banish her from my shop, from my household. She has been a disruptive influence from the beginning; she has tried to corrupt my children, blight my blossoms." Her voice trailed off to a bleat as the man gestured her to silence.

"Who told you the secret?" asked the man, turning to Clever-Lazy. "Who betrayed the Emperor? It was the tax collector, wasn't it? I shall see that he gets into trouble for this!"

Clever-Lazy chose her words slowly as she probed into the past. "I remember that tax collector," she said. "He came to our village, and I showed him the counting device. You have it all backwards. First, I played with the beans, then I learned to sort and count them. Then, in a flash, I saw how to place them in rows as I have done here. But the beans rolled all over the place and I asked my parents for wooden beads. I threaded them onto rods, and I asked my father to make a frame to hold them in place. I wanted to be able to slide the beads, you see, without losing them or getting the columns mixed up."

"But who told you how to put the right number of beans into columns in the first place? Was it your father?"

"Oh, no!" replied Clever-Lazy, shocked. "My father was a busy, hardworking man. He never had time to play. He never could have devised such a system. It took someone lazy, like me, to do that."

"Do you mean to say that it was you, a mere child, a mere *girl* child, who devised such a . . . such a brilliant and complicated instrument?" asked the man.

"But my abacus was just one of many devices," rejoined Clever-Lazy. "I *like* to invent things. The tax collector was a nice little man, but if you had been about and had let me sit under the village tree with you, I would just as likely have given it to you."

"I honestly believe you would have," he said. Amusement as well as admiration glinted in his eyes. "Ah, well. Just my luck. It's too late now and the harm's done. Ideas like that come once in a thousand years."

"I have ideas like that almost every day," said Clever-Lazy.

9

The Proposition

HIS NAME, HE told them, was Ascending One. He had come to buy a dozen of the new teapots that were the talk of the court. He took pride, he said, in the selection and presentation of discreet gifts. Shopshrewd took one of the teapots from the shelf and placed it on the counter. "The right gift at the right time, honorable sir," she murmured.

Ascending One ran his finger along the curved spout. Abruptly he turned to Clever-Lazy. "Girl, did you invent this? Prove to me that a spout with a bulge is better than a short, straight spout."

Clever-Lazy took pleasure in explaining the principle of the steam trap to him. Perhaps because he listened so attentively, she surprised herself by adding, "The next shipment will have a small improvement. Instead of a full opening from the body of the pot into the spout, there will be little holes. The holes will filter out the tea leaves." There! The idea had been growing in her head for days, but it was not until this instant that she had let it rise to the surface.

Ascending One said he would take a pot for his wife, and he reserved the right to buy all the first shipment if the new design met with his approval. He wanted to be the only one at court with access to what he was certain most people would covet. "What else do you have that's new and that I should know about?" he asked Clever-Lazy.

Clever-Lazy showed him the copper kettle that Tinker had left on consignment. Ascending One admired the workmanship as well as the design. He agreed to the delay and ordered half a dozen. As she was returning the kettle to the shelf, Clever-Lazy remarked, "Something else that I have been thinking about is steam. The power of steam."

"Power?" asked Ascending One. His nostrils widened. Clever-Lazy thought to herself that he looked rather like a pig.

"Yes, steam power. Have you ever put your hand on a pot lid while water is boiling inside?"

Shopshrewd was tugging at her sleeve. "Zzzzt! The honorable Ascending One does not boil his own rice. He has women and servants to do that for him." She turned to Ascending One. "The girl is talking nonsense," she apologized. "She means well but she daydreams and mixes things up." She added charitably, "She sees things in a different way from you and me."

"I'm sure she does," said Ascending One. His voice was dry as a cricket's. Then he bellowed, "Woman, shut your mouth! Something important is going on! I don't expect you to understand, but I do expect you to keep quiet." He turned back to Clever-Lazy. "Continue, girl. What do you know about the power of steam?"

"Well, for one thing, it pushes. It pushes hard, even the small amount in a kettle. I think about all the people in the world who work hard, about all the animals who push or pull for us, and I wonder if there is some way we could use steam instead." She gave a little giggle. "I know it would look ridiculous, but I wonder what would happen if we put a big kettle on wheels?"

"Girl, what's your name?"

When she told him, he was silent for such a long time that she thought he had not heard her. "Clever-Lazy! The name's a paradox. Yet, 'Opposing forces yield much energy.'" Again he fell silent. Only the three middle fingers of his right hand made an almost noiseless tune as he tapped them on the counter. He turned to Shopshrewd.

"I want to make a proposition, a business proposition," he said. "I want to remove this young woman from your care to my own compound. For your inconvenience I shall reimburse you, of course." He shot a glance at Shopshrewd. "Within reason, of course. In return I expect utmost secrecy."

Shopshrewd bowed low. "As the honorable Ascending One wishes. Surely you must know that you can trust me." Her voice turned squeaky with excitement. "Just give me a little time, a week or two, to prepare the girl for the great honor you have bestowed."

Ascending One ignored her and turned to Clever-Lazy.

"Do you understand me, girl? I want you to come and live under my protection. You will have a shed in the corner of my compound that I will make suitable for your work. No one will be allowed to bother you while you perfect your inventions. You can be as lazy and clever as your heart desires as long as you produce results with which I can please and amuse the Emperor. But whatever you do must be just for me. Now tell me what you need."

Clever-Lazy hardly dared pay attention to the flood of pure joy that threatened to engulf her. "Is water nearby?" she asked. "May I have a crucible? What about charcoal? I'll need scales, mortars, pestles. From time to time, there will be special equipment, special tools that I will design and have made. And oh, yes, rare plants, rare minerals . . ."

Shopshrewd was staring at her in astonishment, almost awe. She opened her mouth. Ascending One waved her to silence. "I believe we understand each other, young woman," he said to Clever-Lazy. "I will draw up a contract that I will expect both you and your aunt to sign. Now I must get back to the palace, but as soon as possible I shall have your new quarters made ready for you." He opened the blue door and stepped into the street. "I shall be back here a week from today at the Hour of the Turtle. See that you are ready!"

Clever-Lazy followed him out to the street; the better to bid farewell and thank him. She bowed deeply. By the time she looked up, Ascending One was already striding down the Street of Kettles. She watched as he shook off an old beggar who often sat in the doorway there and who had run out to clutch his sleeve. Ascending One kicked at him and missed. "A week from today," Clever-Lazy called after him, suddenly afraid the whole thing was a dream.

"At the Hour of the Turtle," he called out, pausing at the end of the street. Then he turned a corner and was gone.

The moment Clever-Lazy reentered the shop, Shopshrewd rushed upon her. "You hussy," she screamed. "You deceitful little hussy!" Clever-Lazy's eyes widened in astonishment. "Don't play the stupid country girl with *me*! I took you into my household thinking you were a virtuous maiden, hardly more than a child, but now I see you are skilled in the wiles of catching rich old men."

"Whatever do you mean?" demanded Clever-Lazy. Then, as understanding dawned, "Do you believe that I would sell my body to such as he? If that be true, then shame on you for encouraging him and for agreeing to accept money from him!" Clever-Lazy's eyes blazed.

Shopshrewd grew suddenly apologetic. "Oh, Clever-Lazy, I did not mean to offend you. Be sure you get everything you mentioned in the contract – a pavilion, the jewels and perfumes. Clever-Lazy, I shall never understand you!"

"You don't begin to understand," said Clever-Lazy.

Shopshrewd prattled on. "Everything bodes well. You will become Ascending One's favorite, and soon even his wife will be in your shadow. When Little Prune is older, you can introduce her to Ascending One's son. Prickle will be managing the shop by then and can benefit by any business you send his way. And P'loy, my precious P'loy, will no doubt find himself at court. Oh, just a lowly position at first. But with his charm and your influence, he will go far."

Clever-Lazy sought to make her voice a solid rock in a babbling stream. "Listen," she said gravely, "my contract with Ascending One has nothing to do with my becoming his mistress. I will be his inventor. I will have a shed, not a pavilion. The minerals I ask for will not be jewels; they will look to you like ordinary rocks. And the rare plants will not be to make perfume; they will just as likely stink."

"I don't believe you," said Shopshrewd in a small voice. "You are trying to trick me."

"You do me and Ascending One an injustice when you interpret his kindness so grossly. I am sure he is supporting an inventor not for personal gratification, but for the glory of the Emperor and for the good of the people."

Shopshrewd made a clicking sound with her tongue. "Clever-Lazy, you are both more clever and more stupid than I give you credit for. I have maligned you. You are a good girl after all, and your goodness makes you blind. Oh, how you need my help!"

"Your help! Shopshrewd, you know nothing of experimenting nor recording observations."

"Poor child," said the older woman soothingly. "Never fear. Ever Curious and I will be able to accomplish wonders even in a week's time."

"But you are not to tell the neighbors, especially Ever Curious. You were sworn to secrecy!"

"But she is my best friend and every bit as discreet as I

am. Fortunately she sews well and will see that you have the proper clothes. A few robes to start with; then Ascending One will adorn you."

"But the clothes I have are good enough to work in. I need a new jacket come next winter, that is true. No doubt Ascending One will give me an allowance for food and clothes. The less I have to trouble myself about, the better."

"And my neighbor's sister, Not Quite," continued Shopshrewd. "She will know what can be done with you. She will show you how to walk, how to sit, how best to serve your master. She is not quite a courtesan herself, but she helps many courtesans dress their hair, and will help with yours. She will know how to pluck your eyebrows and where to purchase kohl, rice powder and vermilion."

Two spots almost as red as vermilion appeared on Clever-Lazy's cheeks. "Shopshrewd, listen to me! The main reason I came to stay with you is because that was the wish of my parents. The other reason was that my friend, Tinker, persuaded me that if I lived on the streets, I might become the kind of silly, wanton girl who paints away her feelings with rice powder and sells her favors to men. Tinker brought me to you because he thought you were respectable and would guard me from such a life."

Shopshrewd found her voice. "A common girl of the streets cannot be compared to the mistress of an important man."

"I find them difficult to compare because I see so little difference," returned Clever-Lazy. "I shall wait until Tinker comes and ask his opinion."

"What does a tinker know about respectability?" asked Shopshrewd scornfully. "Ascending One would be most upset if he found out about your friendship with a common tinker. You must never mention him again."

"He is not a common tinker. Actually, he is an uncommon one! Ascending One was impressed by the workmanship shown in his kettle. The first thing I shall do is tell Ascending One that I intend to ask Tinker to marry me."

Shopshrewd gave a strangled cry. "Oh, you wicked ungrateful girl! And now you would ruin me and my children besides. I should take the advice of Ever Curious and sell you to the House of Flowers!" She flew at Clever-Lazy like an angry cat, and would have scratched her face if she had not suddenly remembered that face was valuable.

The noise of the argument had attracted the children. Little Prune ran next door to bring Ever Curious, who came even more promptly than usual. As Shopshrewd poured out her grievances, Clever-Lazy withdrew to a far corner of the shop.

After a while, she found herself staring at a shaft of sunlight that fell on a glazed bowl. A blue dragon floated like a cloud on the convex surface. A wavy blue border around the foot of the bowl suggested to her the far-off mountains of her childhood. She thought of her home and village; she remembered the day when she and her parents climbed to the sanctuary of the Goddess. For the first time in months, she prayed.

"O Goddess! Tell me what to do."

Gradually the sunlight shifted and the bowl was left in shadow. *But the dragon continued to float.*

"Thank you, Goddess," whispered Clever-Lazy. Now she knew what to do. She would float and watch and be aware, ready to act when the time came.

10

A Mere Doll

FOR THREE DAYS the Shop of the Blue Door was closed to the public. Clever-Lazy was instructed to paint the character for "Closed" on the door, and the three women set about their self-imposed task of making Clever-Lazy presentable.

Only on the first day did the sign fail. They were interrupted by a knock and a determined rattling. A harsh voice bawled out, "Let me in, you silly fools! It's me, Bowlmaker!" The latch leaped its hasp, and she managed to open the door a crack.

"What's going on in there? What are you doing to that girl?" Bowlmaker demanded. She stared hard at Not Quite, not pleased with what she saw. Shopshrewd flew at her and pushed her out, closing the door hard. She leaned her back against it while Ever Curious secured the lock, and Bowlmaker continued to shout and bang.

Finally, grumbling, Bowlmaker went away. Ever Curious, peering through a slit, reported that she had stopped to speak to the old beggar at the corner. She saw the old man hold up his hand, count his fingers and point to the Blue Door. Then she saw him miming a pompous mandarin who suddenly kicked at something (or someone) in the dust. He and Bowlmaker disappeared together around the corner.

Shopshrewd had lugged hot water, enough to fill a tub. Clever-Lazy was doused and scrubbed like a small child. At length, she was permitted to clothe herself in a loose shift. She was ordered to sit on a low stool so that Not Quite could pull out her eyebrows hair by hair. Clever-Lazy wriggled and yelped and told herself she should have run away days ago while she still had the chance. Then she remembered the promise of a workshop of her own. She tried to picture it, item by item. She became so immersed in planning the perfect workshop that she was surprised when Not Quite released her.

Not Quite asked for a scarf and used it to tie back Clever-Lazy's hair, exposing the full forehead. She began to apply a paste of rice powder. Clever-Lazy felt her skin pull and tighten. "What happens if I laugh or cough?" she asked, through barely moving lips.

"You are not allowed to laugh or cough," retorted Not Quite. She pulled the scarf from Clever-Lazy's head and inspected her hair gravely. Ever Curious whined apologies.

"I brushed and brushed until my arms ached. It's not my fault if the hair is not to your liking."

"The hair is all right," returned Not Quite. "Those who have pink cheeks often as not have good hair. This is thick and shiny. Look!" She held up and let fall a fan of black silk. Clever-Lazy winced as she combed, then winced at the wincing. The white mask had tightened every part of her face.

"Stop making faces," ordered Not Quite, not unkindly. She began to coil and tug, loop and fold Clever-Lazy's hair into an elaborate construction that hid her ears, pulled at her nape and burdened her brow. The other women murmured their admiration.

Not Quite stepped back to better assess Clever-Lazy, as if she were an object to be decorated. She seized a thin brush and a small jar and painted two curved lines high above the ridge of Clever-Lazy's brow. The new eyebrows gave her a look of sustained surprise. With the same black substance Not Quite rimmed Clever-Lazy's eyes, causing them to sting. Next she took a new brush and a cake of vermilion. She put a round red circle on each cheek. Finally she painted the mouth, leaving out the corners. Clever-Lazy's mouth looked like a red "O" poised in astonishment.

Clever-Lazy *was* astonished. 'Why are these women doing this to me?' she wondered.

At last it was time to don the new dress. Ever Curious brought in the garment, which she had been working on day and night. There was not time enough nor money for rich embroidery, much less embroidered silk. Nevertheless Clever-Lazy found herself exclaiming with pleasure over the dull rich glow of earth-red homespun, bordered with a band of woven iris that ran diagonally from her right shoulder down to the hem.

"Oh, Ever Curious, how beautiful! How clever you are!" she exclaimed. She flung her arms around her and kissed her.

"Hmmph!" grunted Ever Curious, pleased in spite of herself. "Such a problem, that girl! She eats too much. I had to cut on the diagonal to make the material do its best by her. I can only hope that the eye of Ascending One will be fooled." Her eyes glinted with pride and appreciation as she helped to button the neck circlet and adjust the deep cuffs. Shopshrewd slipped high-soled clogs onto Clever-Lazy's feet. Clever-Lazy swayed precariously, trying to balance.

"I never would have believed it," exulted Not Quite. "There is hardly any trace of that miserable lump we started with."

"I can never thank you enough," returned Shopshrewd. "I never could have done it without your help. Together the three of us have wrought a miracle."

"Miracle!" grumbled Ever Curious. "Hard work is what's done it. I've strained my eyes and pricked my fingers raw trying to get that robe finished in time. I'd go home and sleep if it were not that I want to be here when Ascending One comes. I plan to hide in the kitchen and peek out so I can see his face."

"He won't recognize her," said Shopshrewd.

Clever-Lazy stole a look in the mirror that Not Quite had not quite stolen from one of the courtesans. It was true. She no longer looked like herself.

What if Ascending One took one look at her and decided that such a fashionable doll was not capable of being an inventor. Or what if he took one look and decided that what he wanted after all was a mere doll? Which would be worse: to be rejected as a mere doll or to be accepted as one?

A tear stung at the corner of Clever-Lazy's eye. She blinked it away and glanced around the shop, trying to find something concrete, familiar, comforting. Her eyes came to rest on the blue bowl. She could see the dragon half hidden by the curve. "I am a dragon and I can float where I choose . . . I am a dragon, far removed and powerful. One blast of my nostrils and those women will scatter . . ."

There was a commotion at the door. A man's voice bawled out, "Open up!"

"He's early," said Not Quite. "The Hour of the Turtle has not yet come."

"What should I do?" asked Shopshrewd, suddenly terrified.

"Well don't just stand there," hissed Ever Curious. "Open the door."

"Open up! I know you are in there!" came the man's voice again. It was hard to hear it through the banging on the door, the rattling of the lock.

"I shall just float and observe," the dragon whispered to herself. "If I don't like what's happening, I'll fly away to the Dancing Mountains." Someone gave the door a kick.

Not Quite turned scarlet with suppressed laughter. "Whoever would think that old man would be so eager!" She shook and choked and wiped her eyes, waving Shopshrewd to the front of the shop.

Shopshrewd crept forward, reached out a trembling hand and lifted the latch just as someone applied the full force of his shoulder to the door. The door was flung open and Tinker burst into the shop, Bowlmaker behind him.

Clever-Lazy saw Tinker burst through the door. She tottered toward him on her high clogs, lost her balance and fell full length. He, too, sprawled forward on the floor. They reached out toward one another but could not quite touch. Clever-Lazy's companions squealed and cried out, then rushed to kick and pummel the interlopers, falling over the stretched-out figures in their eagerness. Bowlmaker scrambled to her feet and leaped into the fray, yelling encouragement both to Tinker and Clever-Lazy. Soon she was fighting and pulling hair with Not Quite. As though by infection, Shopshrewd and Ever Curious began to quarrel.

In the confusion, Tinker managed to crawl closer to Clever-Lazy. For a moment their fingers touched. Clever-Lazy tried to move closer to him, too, but someone was standing on the hem of her dress. She did manage to sit up and soon the two of them were sitting in the middle of the floor, their arms around each other. When Ascending One arrived, he paused in astonishment at the door. "What is going on here?" he thundered.

All eyes turned to him. Tinker scrambled to his feet, faced the newcomer and flung out his arms, shielding Clever-Lazy. Shopshrewd gave a moan of grief and terror. The eyes of Ever Curious widened even more than usual as she backed toward the kitchen. She almost fell over Not Quite, who was edging in the same direction. Clever-Lazy had slipped out of her clogs and was trying to stand and face Ascending One, although she was half-hidden by Tinker. Tinker finally found his voice.

"You can't have her," he cried out. "Not if I have to die defending her!"

"Whatever is he talking about?" asked Ascending One to no one in particular. Tinker waved a fist under his nose.

"You can't have her."

"Young man, pray put down your fist," said Ascending One, his voice a trifle weary. "Perhaps, under these circumstances, I don't even want her."

At this, Clever-Lazy cried out, "Aiee! But that's not fair. You promised!"

Tinker swerved around to face her, astonishment and consternation showing in every line of his body. He was taken so off balance that, for a moment, he almost collapsed on the floor again. He regained himself in time, but stood open mouthed as Clever-Lazy continued to address Ascending One. Her eyes were blazing, and she stamped a bare foot.

"You promised me a place of my own. Oh, don't refuse to take me now! I've made wonderful plans and I know I can please you."

Tinker gave a low moan and put his arm up to his face as though warding off a blow, but Bowlmaker stepped closer to Clever-Lazy and touched her sleeve. "Tell me, little one, what sort of place did the man promise?" Ascending One started to speak but she waved him to silence.

"A workshop. A workshop of my very own with retorts and mortars and scales and measuring devices," replied Clever-Lazy. She fought back a sob.

"And what were you and this . . . this honorable gentleman planning to accomplish together?" Tinker raised his head, listening despite himself.

"I would be his inventor. In return, he would grant me time and space. I would let him use whatever I invent, and since he works for the Emperor, I am sure he would let the Emperor know about my work. And the Emperor would decide how to use my inventions for the benefit of the people. And now I'll never have the chance!"

Sooty kohl and tears made gray streaks down Clever-Lazy's whitened face. She gave a great wail and fell into Bowlmaker's arms. Bowlmaker held her close, patting her shoulder.

"There, there," she said. "Men were ever cruel deceivers." Her scornful glance took in both men present.

Ascending One was first to speak. "The girl is painted like a poppet," he declared. "Who is responsible for this nonsense?"

Clever-Lazy's voice cut through the babble of blame and counter-blame. "I am," she said. "No one can make me do something I don't want to do. I could have refused or run away, but I will do anything in order to become an inventor. I want my own workshop."

Tinker had been listening carefully. Now he blurted out, "What do you mean, that you would do anything? Have you no shame?"

Clever-Lazy turned toward him, her eyes steadfast. "I can only corrupt myself," she said.

"You are either foolish or courageous – or ruthless," said Ascending One. He seemed amused. But Tinker was not amused. He took her hand and looked into her eyes.

"Marry me," he said. "You need me to look after you. I promise to make you happy."

Clever-Lazy smiled at him with such piercing sweetness that he felt his heart jump. "I want to marry you, Tinker, and I will. But I don't want you to look after me. As for making me happy, no one else can do that for me. Not even you."

Tinker sighed. "Then marry me and look after me," he pleaded. "Make *me* happy."

Clever-Lazy giggled. The sound of that dear and familiar giggle reminded Tinker of all the quarrels and reconciliations they had had in the past. "Look after a tinker?" she asked. "You wander the roads alone, you know the streets, you face all weathers and people and conditions. You don't need someone to look after you! Nor can *I* make *you* happy. You must do that yourself." She reached out a hand and touched his cheek. "Oh, Tinker, I do love you so! Yes, I will marry you as soon as Ascending One gives me my workshop."

Ascending One gave a small dry cough. "Let me be the first to congratulate you, young man. If you had not appeared, I would have had to marry the young woman off to one of my servants." He turned to Bowlmaker. Her kerchief had fallen off, her hair had become unbraided and one sleeve was torn. Nevertheless, Ascending One said, "You look like the most respectable woman here. Do you think you can arrange a wedding on short notice?"

"That I can do," said Bowlmaker, "but do not forget that this young woman is not without family. Shopshrewd is her father's cousin's wife, and Clever-Lazy should be married from her household. I shall be happy to assist but let us leave no room for misunderstanding. Respectability above all else!"

"Respectability!" echoed Tinker, his face brightening.

"Above all else!" chorused Ascending One. Again he spoke to Tinker. "My one hesitancy about setting up a workshop for Clever-Lazy has been that she is an attractive young woman without a husband. My wife warned me that people would misconstrue my intentions. And I see that they have." The three women huddled at the other end of the shop cowered beneath his glance.

Tinker bowed. "Oh, honorable sir," he said. "We cannot thank you enough. I wish to apologize to you, sir. I have harbored unjust and evil thoughts —"

Ascending One put a hand to stay him. "Enough! Let us make this clear once and for all: What I want from

Clever-Lazy is the absolute right to her inventions. I am buying her mind, not her body."

Tinker's face lit up with joy. "Clever-Lazy! Do you hear that? The honorable Ascending One does not want you for evil purposes. He only wants to buy your mind!"

Clever-Lazy felt a cold chill sweep through her, but the next moment she was surrounded by an excited hubbub of congratulations on her coming marriage.

11

The Inventor

CLEVER-LAZY AND TINKER lived in a tumble-down house that stood within the compound of Ascending One. The people of the court referred to them as Inventor and Inventor's husband.

Although it lay near the palace, Ascending One's compound was not actually part of the royal household. Accordingly, he and his followers were not supplied from the Emperor's table, but were supported by Ascending One's own barnyard and carp pond and from a vegetable patch beyond, by the river. Inventor's house was attached to a cattle byre that, in turn, abutted a pig sty. Inventor and her husband thought they were as near to heaven as human beings can possibly be.

Clever-Lazy and Tinker never seemed to find time to furnish their quarters like other people. Somewhere in the shadows was a roll of quilts for the two of them to sleep on. Not infrequently, at the end of the day, they had to search for it because it might have disappeared beneath an avalanche of other articles.

Their one table, meant for dining, was burdened with such a collection of rocks and bones and fossils and dried roots and jars of strange-smelling liquids and colored powders that more often than not, they ate their meals under the cherry tree in the courtyard. Since they liked being outdoors, and delighted in watching ducks and chickens and other farmyard animals, the arrangement suited them. Or if they were busy, as often happened, they ate when they felt like it while standing over their work.

The collection on the table continued onto the floor and was merely the overflow from the shelves that lined the walls. Along one shelf was a collection of eggs arranged according to size (linnet to dinosaur); along another, shells (limpet to giant conch), and on another a row of skulls (mouse to man to mastodon). An earthen bowl held lumps of yellow amber, which glowed like fire coals. Next to the bowl were placed chunks of iron and magnetite and, next to that, a piece of rock said to come from a falling star. These unlike objects especially puzzled Clever-Lazy because they shared a common ability to attract other objects, mustard seeds and iron filings, although they did not attract the same things in the same way.

Overhead a collection of birds' wings hung from the ceiling. These Clever-Lazy had strung up so she could observe how they responded to air currents and contemplate their marvelous structure. Bunches of herbs hung from the rafters as well as strange-shaped roots. A dried crocodile peered down from where it was wedged near the ceiling; a giant tortoise shell hung on one wall and a cobra skin was pegged to another. In one corner was heaped a collection of horns, tusks and teeth: narwhal, shark, mammoth, walrus, rhinoceros, elephant and unicorn.

Shopshrewd came to visit several times after the marriage and went away bitter and baffled. She had thought that her relative would be living in a pavilion at court; instead she lived next to a cowshed. She had expected that Clever-Lazy would elevate her relatives to wealth and social position, and blamed Clever-Lazy for the death of her hopes. Worst of all, Shopshrewd could not understand why Clever-Lazy and the tinker were so happy. They lived like pigs, she said, in a clutter of objects fit only for the dung heap.

Shopshrewd reported to Ever Curious that Clever-Lazy had actually invented ways to be lazier than ever. Unlike any self-respecting, decent woman who ran to the well each time she needed water, Clever-Lazy had had Tinker construct a cistern on the roof of their hovel. From this reservoir ran a system of troughs and bamboo pipes that carried water to a gigantic kettle held in suspension in a wooden frame built just under the roof. Beneath this monster they kept an almost perpetual fire so that the water was always hot. Even more self-indulgent and shocking, Clever-Lazy had designed a flexible copper tube that curved from the hot water tank toward a basin. All she had to do when she needed hot water was to turn a little handle!

Clever-Lazy did not consider her house cluttered or untidy, nor did her husband. The objects on the shelves were sorted and categorized as carefully as she had sorted out beans and seeds in the old days. Everything in the workshop was labeled and catalogued and given a number. Every day Clever-Lazy observed and recorded what she was doing. Her only uneasiness was caused by Ascending One, who did not seem to understand that Clever-Lazy thought it more important to observe the laws of nature than to devise some toy or novelty for him to exhibit at court.

One night, Ascending One was awakened by an explosion coming from his courtyard. Half dressed, he ran into the yard to find Clever-Lazy sitting by the well calmly writing notes.

"Inventor! What's happened?" he cried.

Clever-Lazy showed him what she had written: "To make a sound like thunder in a copper vessel, put boiling water into such a vessel and then sink it in a well. It will make a loud noise."

"But what's it good for?" asked Ascending One. "Besides waking up the neighborhood," he added.

"First I must see what happened to the teakettle," said Clever-Lazy. She bent over the well and hauled up something by a piece of rope. "Tinker, look at that!" she exulted. Ascending One found himself staring at the remains of a teakettle, its sides crumpled almost beyond recognition. Even Tinker was puzzled.

"What do you think happened to it?" he asked.

Clever-Lazy consulted her notes. "I clamped the lid tight and I stuffed up the spout with clay. The kettle was full of steam when I rushed it to the well and threw it in."

"In the middle of the night?" asked Ascending One.

"At night the water is at its coldest." She turned to Tinker. "By cooling the kettle suddenly I guess we caused the steam to condense. It sort of squeezed in on itself and left an empty space, a vacuum. The sides of the kettle fell inward. That means there was an *im*plosion, not an *ex*plosion. I suppose the wall of the well made an echo. That's where the noise like thunder came from."

She giggled. "I'm sorry, Ascending One. I didn't mean to wake you, nor wake your neighbors. But just think of the energy that was locked up in that steam! I've found a way to release it, and that's what I've been searching for."

Ascending One sighed and tried to stifle a yawn. He scratched the back of his neck thoughtfully. "I still don't see the use of all this," he said. "When we made our agreement, I was led to believe that you were on the verge of discovering the secret of power and that when you did, *I* would gain more power."

"But what we just heard was power," Clever-Lazy argued. "You saw the teapot yourself. It looks as though it has been crumpled by a dragon's claw. Now if we could only figure out how to control that energy, make it flow where we want it to, push and pull . . ."

"Enough, enough," sighed Ascending One. Now he was trying to scratch between his shoulder blades. In sympathy, Tinker offered him his own backscratcher, a bamboo stick almost as long as an arm with a span of apple twigs stuck into one hollow end. The twigs were like the fingers on a hand.

"What's that?" demanded Ascending One suspiciously.

Tinker showed him how to use it. "Clever-Lazy made it for me. When I am working at my furnace, the heat makes my back itch. I used to call for her to come and scratch me." He laughed, put his arm around his wife's waist and gave her a little pinch. "We all know she is lazy, but she is also clever. So she invented this for me."

Ascending One took the bamboo stick from his hand and applied it between his own shoulder blades. A look of absolute bliss settled over his usually wary countenance. "Ahhhh!" he sighed. Then, "Ohhh! Inventor, *this* is the kind of thing you should spend your time inventing!" He held it out so he could look at it. "Such a simple idea — yet it works like magic! We must make a more elegant model and present it to the Emperor. How about a gold backscratcher?"

"Metal is too harsh on the skin," said Clever-Lazy. "I suggest you try ivory, Honorable Ascending One." She took her brush and scroll and quickly let flow a design. "Have the ivory carver make the scratching end look like an actual human hand with fingers slightly curved. So! He could even place a jewelled ring on one finger as further proof of your esteem. Perhaps a small ruby? Be sure to ask a fortune-teller how to carve good luck and long life into the lines in the palm of the hand."

Clever-Lazy rolled up the piece of paper and gave it to her patron, then took the backscratcher into her own hand. Thoughtfully she balanced it and sighted down its length. (No one knew it at the time, but she was about to invent the piston engine). She held the bamboo rod straight out in front of her and started to push it back and forth, bending her elbow in rhythmical but rather jerky strokes. "I am thinking," she said on the forward thrust, "that this might be" (return), "just what we need" (forward), "to use steam power" (return), "to push" (forward), "and pull" (return).

She let her arm drop and held up the battered kettle in her other hand. "Oh, Tinker, you are so clever! With your help I'm going to be able to make some metal arms, each with a cylinder attached. Each of the cylinders will make a little explosion . . ."

From behind them came the voice of Ascending One. "Inventor, I forbid you to spend any more time on such nonsense. You are gifted and you are clever, and I bought you and your ideas in order to help me rise at court. I want you to make toys and useful objects that will please the Emperor." He appealed to Tinker. "Surely you must see that as I ascend, so will you and your wife. You must teach your wife to obey orders."

Tinker gently removed the kettle from Clever-Lazy's hand. "Listen to the honorable Ascending One," he counseled in a voice loud enough for their patron to hear. "It behooves us to know and understand his wishes just as it behooves him to comprehend the wishes of the Emperor." He bowed low to Ascending One and tugged at Clever-Lazy's sleeve until she followed suit.

So it was that Clever-Lazy did not invent the piston engine, although she was very near to doing so. The Emperor was presented with a jewelled ivory backscratcher, when he could have had a steam engine or a steamship or a silk mill run on steam power. Since he never knew what he was missing, he was pleased with his gift (part tool, part toy) and called for more novelties like it.

12

Toys for the Emperor

ASCENDING ONE WAS certain that there were articles lying about Inventor's workshop that for some mischievous reason she was determined to keep secret. He came into the workshop and rummaged about with no awareness of the destruction he was causing. As Clever-Lazy explained to Tinker, the separate objects were not as important as their relationship to one another. Once their order was disturbed, an idea that was still in the hatching state could be lost forever.

Thus it was one sunny morning Ascending One came upon a prism, a triangular chunk of glass, which reflected many colors. He carried it off without so much as by-your-leave to show to the Emperor. The Emperor was delighted to own a piece of rainbow.

The next day Ascending One presented the Emperor with a magnifying glass, also "borrowed" from his inventor.

He showed the Emperor how he could look at what was very tiny (an ant, a grain of sand, the texture of his robe), and perceive it as being much larger. The Emperor sat in the sunlight with his prism in one hand and his magnifying glass in the other, turning and twisting them to catch the light. To his dismay, and much to the consternation of Ascending One, the sunlight turned the magnifier into a burning glass, scorched a tiny hole through the Emperor's silk robe and burned the Imperial knee.

The next time Ascending One came to court, he brought Clever-Lazy with him in order that she might instruct the Emperor in the uses of his gifts. Inventor brought a lump of amber from her sleeve, rubbed it and showed the Emperor how it could attract particles of straw and mustard seeds. She then brought out a piece of magnetized iron, and showed how it could pick up or be attracted by anything else with iron in it.

The Emperor was enchanted. He invited her to come to court one evening to entertain the lords and ladies there. Inventor brought a saucer and a little wooden fish, which had a piece of the magnetized iron embedded in its head, and a needle sticking out of its mouth. She filled the saucer with water and set the little fish afloat. As though it were alive, the fish turned of its own accord so that the needle in its mouth pointed to the north star. However she maneuvered the saucer, the little fish always turned loyally to the north again. The whole court marveled at the toy. Clever-Lazy had invented the compass.

The lords and ladies invited Inventor to go hunting with them. She noticed that when the Emperor pulled up on his horse, the snorting stallion was almost choked to death by the bridle strap that crossed his windpipe. She designed a new harness for the Imperial hunting horses and, on the Emperor's urging, improved the harness for all beasts of burden. Now the animals took strain at the chest instead of across the throat.

She also invented stirrups. With them the Emperor could better wheel his horse and control it as he rode. This left his hands free to use another of Inventor's inventions, the crossbow. She invented a cross-lined sight for the crossbow so that the Emperor could aim with hairbreadth precision.

The Emperor decreed that a pleasure dome be built for him, but the workmen were slow and the Emperor fretted. Inventor designed a new kind of hod for the masons to carry stones, a barrow with a wheel in the center of it and handles to guide and tip the load. The workers complained that when the wind was strong, they had to run to keep up. She added more wheels to the barrow and a sail. She hoped a man could sit in it and sail along the road, but the vehicle was too clumsy to maneuver on land. Clever-Lazy sighed and thought of her ideas for using steam.

Thinking of steam, she wondered if it could be used to turn a paddle wheel on a boat. Instead she invented a system of paddles and pedals that could be worked by the feet, and installed the device in the Imperial pleasure barge. The Emperor enjoyed being transported about the palace lake with more privacy and less fuss than when the boat was rowed or under sail. Until he tired of the novelty, he spent long hours on the lake trailing his hands in the water while one of the little concubines sang and played the lute for him.

While the Emperor was dabbling his hand in the lake, Clever-Lazy and Tinker were sweating over a new blast furnace she had designed. The new furnace was fanned to an intense heat by a giant bellows, which was worked through a system of belts and connecting rods powered by the river. The first thing Tinker manufactured was a chain-link iron bridge that was suspended across a gorge high in the mountains. In perfect safety, the Emperor was able to walk back and forth and look at the view. He wrote a poem about it that was much admired by the court.

The inventor commissioned the jade carvers to make a hollow tube pierced with clear, cut designs. When warm air was forced through the tube, there was a roaring sound and the tube, suspended over a lamp, turned round and round. Shadows of galloping horses, chariots, armies, forests were thrown against the wall. The Emperor caught his breath in fear and wonder. When the lamp was extinguished, the roaring sound stopped and the ghostly army disappeared. Only then did the Emperor breathe naturally again.

Meanwhile, Tinker had been engaged in the manu-facture of a dozen iron figures: men, women, birds, beasts.

These puppets were marvelously jointed and hinged so that they could be made to bow and strut, flap their wings or hit a gong. The whole company was worked with a system of levers, pulleys, chains, belts, wheels and fly wheels that operated on water power. With the help of Tinker, Clever-Lazy added a pendulum and weights. She added a painted dial that showed the hours and minutes of the day, the weeks and months of the year, the equinoxes and the solstices, the phases of the moon.

The Emperor was enchanted until, of course, he became bored. He complained that the hands on the dials too often repeated themselves; the puppets always did the same thing.

Remembering her own beloved puppets, Clever-Lazy was sympathetic. She commissioned puppets to be made not of dough but of ivory. The cast of characters included an Emperor and Empress, priests and chancellors, warriors and foot soldiers. They all moved about on a little stage to tell any story one could make up. The Emperor was delighted as long as Clever-Lazy sat by his side and whispered stories into his ear, but when she was not with him, he was incapable of thinking up plots by himself.

With the Emperor's permission, Inventor took the little theater back to her workshop. She had a duplicate set of characters made, this time of jet. She had the square stage marked off into sixty-four alternate squares, half black, half white. She wrote out a handbook of suggested moves to show how the two sets of pieces could combine and contend. She had invented the game of chess.

The Emperor was still unhappy. What would he do once he had worked out all the moves possible? Clever-Lazy spent a whole day calculating so that she could reassure him. When she was ready, the Emperor summoned a scribe. The scribe unrolled a long scroll and dipped his brush in the ink. Then, as Inventor dictated, he wrote the characters for: 169,518,829,100,544,000,000,000,000,000. That, she explained, was the number of ways possible to play the first ten moves.

The Emperor loved his new game, but he did not want anyone to watch his face while he played it. Especially, he did not want anyone to see his expression when he lost. Clever-Lazy presented him with a pair of rose-colored spectacles ground from purple quartz.

Inventor presented the Emperor with a kaleidoscope, a tube with mirrors glued into it at angles. Pieces of quartz crystal and loose glass were enclosed in the tube. Every time the tube was shaken, these bits and pieces were reflected in the little mirrors. The tube had a small hole at one end so the Emperor could peek in. The number of patterns he could make by a shake of his hand was infinite. The kaleidoscope was a success.

The next few inventions were not.

Clever-Lazy worked with Tinker to produce a mirror that would project an image that was carved on the back of it. The reflecting side was made of white bronze. The other side was darker. All of the tinker's skill and all of the inventor's knowledge of light and refraction went into the making of the marvelous mirror.

The outer layer of the mirror back was carved with the figure of a dragon. An inner layer was carefully carved and calculated to take advantage of interfering light beams. When the Emperor looked into the reflecting side of the mirror, he saw his own round, familiar face. When the mirror was held at a certain angle, in strong sunlight, the dragon carved on the other side seemed to leap out to be reflected on a wall or screen.

The Emperor did not like his new mirror. He could not understand the principle of interferometry, and he felt a small chill at the appearance of the dragon. He wondered if it were his duty to suspect sorcery.

Inventor pounded oyster shells to extract their phosphorous, then pounded the phosphorous into a fine powder that she worked into an ink stick. She painted a picture for the Emperor that, by day, showed an ox standing in a field with a barnyard and byre behind. At night, the picture shone in the dark. Even more wonderful, the ox no longer stood in the field but knelt in its byre. Of course, what Clever-Lazy had done was to paint two pictures, one over the other. The ordinary paint showed by day, the phosphorous paint by night. The Emperor said nothing, but he was aware of a prickle at the back of his neck whenever he saw the picture glow. He ordered a curtain to be placed over it.

Inventor presented the Emperor with a slim tin box filled with pine splinters. Each splinter had been dipped in sulphur and phosphorous. When, at her direction, he scraped one of the splinter heads on a piece of stone, fire burst forth and burned for a few seconds along the length of pine. Startled, he dropped it from his seared fingers. Now he remembered how the magnifying glass had caught the sun and scorched his knee.

The Emperor summoned Ascending One and asked him to ask Inventor to invent something as harmless and infinitely amusing as the kaleidoscope, the last invention he could remember enjoying peacefully. He wanted something just like it only different.

Inventor asked for a room in the palace. She set large mirrors around the room at varying angles. Some curved inward (concave) and reflected the image as larger than it really was. Some curved outward (convex) and made the image shrink. Most of the mirrors had wavy surfaces and were both concave and convex at the same time. Some mirrors turned the image upside down; some split the image in a waistlike effect, narrow at the center and doubled back on itself. Some mirrors made the image appear thinner; others, fatter. Some of the images were grotesque; most would make you laugh.

Clever-Lazy covered the floor of the room with rich carpets of intricate design. She hung the ceiling with brocade and patterned cloth and suspended baskets of flowers. She placed painted bowls and vases where they would catch the light and be reflected in the mirrors. The mirrors reflected and multiplied each others' reflections. When the Emperor and his court, clad in embroidered robes, moved about in the room, the room became as a giant kaleidoscope and they, as pieces of colored quartz, reflected in angled mirrors. With every movement an infinity of new and different patterns was revealed.

The Emperor wondered how he could ever have had doubts about his inventor. He sent for Ascending One to congratulate him on his cleverness in hiring Clever-Lazy. The kaleidoscope room was enchanting, and now he wanted something else just like it only different.

The inventor asked for another room. She had all light sealed off from it. Only one tiny pinprick remained, which allowed a beam of light to enter and shine on the opposite wall. The Emperor was invited to sit in a chair and face the wall where the light was reflected. He was told to watch carefully.

Outside the room, on a stage carefully placed so light shone behind it, Inventor directed a procession of members of the court. Each courtier was instructed to walk into the center of the stage, to turn his or her head, to lift an arm or make some other gesture, then walk off stage. One of the Emperor's concubines even managed a charming little dance.

Inside the room, the Emperor sat in the first camera obscura ever invented. What he saw (and what Clever-Lazy did not anticipate) was a procession of figures turned upside down. As though this were not bad enough, the figures were only a few inches high! The figures, once he got used to seeing them small and upside down, were definitely recognizable. No one, least of all the Emperor, could fail to recognize the features of his Lord High Chancellor, the dignified but disapproving mien of his Empress. What frightened him most of all was the spectacle of the little concubine alive and dancing. This was no puppet, no lamp-shade shadow!

The Emperor felt himself bathed in sweat. What would happen to the world if *he* could be reduced to two inches high and stood upon his head?

13

Corruption

THE EMPEROR INVITED the Emperor of the Southeast to visit him. One of the reasons was that he wanted to show off his toys. I do not mean by this that he wanted to share them. Rather, he wanted to see the gleam of appreciation in another Emperor's eye.

The Emperor sent for Ascending One and ordered him to order his inventor to produce something new and splendid. He specified that he wanted something that could be seen by great crowds of people all at once. He wanted something awesome, spectacular, astonishing, joyful, inspiring and absolutely new. He wanted to be surprised but not too surprised.

Quite frankly, Ascending One was relieved that the Emperor had sent for him. A certain coolness had been exhibited by His Imperial Highness. Surely this new and important commission meant that he, Ascending One, was back in favor. Something of these doubts and hopes he tried to impart to the inventor.

Clever-Lazy listened gravely. Recently, she said, an idea had come to her that might provide exactly what the Emperor wanted. Unfortunately, if the invention were used carelessly, there could be a certain amount of danger.

"Would the Emperor be endangered?" asked Ascending One. When he received reassurance of the Imperial safety, he asked, "Would he be . . . uh . . . upset?" He reminded Inventor of the experience with the camera obscura.

"There will be some loud noises that might upset him if he were not forewarned," Clever-Lazy admitted. "This time I will take care to explain to His Highness beforehand what to expect. I am certain that the noise will seem of small importance when he looks into the night skies and sees the fireworks I shall prepare."

"Fireworks?"

"Flares of light, flying sparks, fountains of fire, fiery dragons, flaming glyphs, flowers of flame . . ." She seemed not to notice the expression of curiosity on her husband's face, excitement and greed on that of her patron.

"I shall detail a gang of men to begin manufacture tomorrow," Ascending One promised eagerly. "Tell me what you need."

Clever-Lazy shook her head. "I am not even sure of the source of ingredients," she said. "What I do know is that the operation is dangerous and must be conducted in secrecy. Once I am finished, I will destroy all records of the process." She turned to Tinker. "Not even you, my love, will know the whole procedure."

Ascending One's nose twitched. Never before had he shown the least interest in how the inventor and the tinker produced the Emperor's toys. Indeed, he turned a deaf ear whenever Clever-Lazy tried to explain to him a principle or a process. Now his inventor had something to hide! What to him was so alarming was Clever-Lazy's very openness about her secrecy. She took full responsibility. Such an assumption of power might well usurp his.

"Be careful," he warned. "Remember I am your patron. Everything you know, everything you learn, belongs to me. I will make the decision as to what should or should not be secret."

During the next few weeks, there came a change in the habits of Clever-Lazy that caused concern to her husband. "She used to smell like warm bread and honey," Tinker told himself, "now she smells like a barnyard."

No wonder she smelled so! She spent most of her time mucking out the pigsty and the cattle byre. When she had scraped the floors, she started on the stone walls, scraping off the scum of years. Once she slipped out of bed at night and Tinker secretly followed her to an old burial ground. He watched fearfully as she scraped away the mold on the grave monuments. When she deposited the substance in a jar and turned toward home, Tinker had to race ahead of her so he could jump under the quilts and pretend to be asleep. The next day she made a little fire in the courtyard and threw the contents of the jar into the flame. A shower of colored sparks snapped and popped as they flew upward.

When Tinker approached her, Clever-Lazy explained that she was looking for an element that was not dangerous in itself, but that would blow up when combined with two other elements. She was afraid that other people would be hurt or killed if anyone else discovered the process or used the product carelessly.

She was looking, she further explained, for a secret source in large amounts and good quality. It existed in the dung of barnyards and in old graves. Tomorrow they would take a picnic to an ancient battlefield and she would test the ground there.

Next day, when they reached the battlefield, Clever-Lazy headed for a low ridge. From there the ground dipped into a water meadow through which rambled a little stream. Here, a hundred years before, two armies had met and fought until the waters ran red with blood. The battle had waged for hours back and forth across the meadow and up the hillside. Bodies had been piled one upon the other. The bodies of the Emperor's soldiers had been reclaimed for honorable burial; the enemy had been stripped of armor and weapons and left to lie under a thin layer of earth.

First Clever-Lazy must test the soil. She made a fire and buried a chunk of iron in the coals. She had brought a spade and dug a hole nearby. When the iron was red hot, she scooped it out of the fire to bury it in the ground. "If the iron turns yellow," she explained to Tinker, "I will know this is the place to dig." Meanwhile, she set a kettle to boil over the fire and blew on the flame. She asked her husband to tend the kettle while she walked down the ridge.

Tinker watched his wife with growing anxiety as she wandered through the meadow. From time to time, he saw her kneel and sniff at the earth. Once, he was almost certain, he saw her actually taste a piece of damp sod, then hurriedly spit it out. Eventually, she came back up the hill, sat down and waited for the kettle. She did not speak.

The tinker served out the meal and watched his wife warily. He thought he had lost her entirely, but when she heard a kingfisher call she turned her head toward the river. She put her finger to her lips and pointed to a flash of blue wing. She smiled at him. It seemed like a long time since she had smiled like that. He did not know he had been holding his breath until he let it out.

"I love you, Clever-Lazy," he said.

"I love you, too." For the first time in weeks, she looked at him, met his eyes. "You look so worried!" she exclaimed. "Your forehead is all puckered." She moved closer to him and smoothed his brow, trying to rub out the furrows. He lay down and put his head in her lap while she continued to stroke his forehead. For an hour or more, they talked and dozed in the spring sunshine.

"Clever-Lazy," he finally blurted out, "why do you spend so much time with death and filth? Surely you can see this is an accursed place?"

"Tinker, I know that terrible things once happened here, but now it's beautiful. I'm trying to make something beautiful for the Emperor. Sometimes beauty comes from corruption. When I dig up that piece of iron, I'll know by its color if this is a place where I can come for the principal element in large amount." She struggled to her feet, went over to where she had dug the hole and felt in the loose earth. She pulled out the piece of iron. It was covered with mottled yellow.

"Just as I hoped!" she crowed. "We can come here often and get what I need. Let me have one of those baskets, Tinker. We'll each take home a barrow full."

As Tinker bent his back over his spade and cut into the rich loam, he felt a prickle of uneasiness run the length of his spine. He uncovered a skull. He looked down at his feet and, as though in a dream, he saw the face of a young soldier of his own age lying on the ground. His eyes stared emptily at Tinker, imploring him to . . . to do what? Tinker shook himself like a dog coming out of water to throw off the vision.

"Clever-Lazy," he pleaded, "this is an evil place. Let us ask Ascending One to send his servants here to do this work. Men died here for no good purpose. Leave them alone, Clever-Lazy, or others will die."

Clever-Lazy hesitated, surprised by the urgency in his voice. "I, too, am afraid others will die. That is why it is so important that I keep the secret to myself. I don't want Ascending One or his men to learn what ingredients I use or how I put them together. Oh, Tinker, if you think I should not proceed, tell me now. I shall tell Ascending One to tell the Emperor that I have decided not to make the new toy."

"It's too late," said Tinker. "Ascending One would be very angry, and we would bring down the wrath of the Emperor. We would lose our workshop and our position at court, and no longer be respectable. Can't you think of something else, Clever-Lazy?"

She shook her head. "There's no time to develop something else. And I can think of nothing comparable to the sensation my fireworks will make. I want so much to please the Emperor, to make him see how clever I am."

Tinker thought again of the young man lying on the battlefield. He shivered. "Death comes from death," he said. "I feel . . . corrupted."

"I feel corrupted, too," agreed Clever-Lazy. Her mood had turned somber. Now she groped for words of comfort. "It will only be for one night in the history of the world," she said. "I'll keep the process secret, Tinker. No one else will ever learn how to make rockets and shells and fireballs and grenades. That I promise you."

The next few days, the inventor banished everyone but herself from the courtyard. She bored a hole in the bottom of her largest wooden washtub, and suspended the tub between two wooden supports so that the contents could drip into a smaller tub placed below. She strewed the bottom of the washtub with straw.

Clever-Lazy mixed earth from the battlefield with the scum and crystals she had collected from the byre walls and grave monuments. She mixed ashes with powdered bone and fossils to make quicklime. She layered soil, straw and quicklime to the brim and then she poured on water, vinegar and urine. For days, a process of dripping, boiling, skimming and reboiling continued, and then she poured the distillation into shallow pans to evaporate. When crystals formed, she stirred them into a fine white powder. 'Everything I've used,' she thought, 'was either dead or burned or rotted.'

In the meantime, Tinker purchased yellow powder from many sources, in small amounts so as not to be noticed. He crushed it, melted it down and purified it to waxy consistency. Then he pressed out its oily essence.

Inventor bought charcoal in many parts of the city. Since charcoal was the common fuel used in every household, this in itself caused no wonder. However, each charcoal burner was given special orders. Wood was to be willow or elder or lime, none other; rotten or pithy or hard, as directed. Rags or paper soaked in various dyes were to be burned along with the wood. Or certain powders (crushed cinnabar, amber, verdigris, scraped ivory) were to be thrown into the flame while the wood and cloth were burning. In all these specifications, she was insistent and severe.

When, at last, enough of these three elements had been produced, Clever-Lazy shut herself up in her workshop away from prying eyes. With delicacy and precision, she ground the elements, mixed them carefully in weighed-out proportion and pressed them together into flat cakes. Then she broke the cakes into grains.

The grains manufactured from ordinary charcoal looked like black peppercorns; the others were colored according to what had been added while making the charcoal. The different colored powders were stored loosely in earthen jars, and the jars were placed in a limestone cave at the bottom of the garden. The place was cool and dark and, at that time of the year, dry.

The secret part of the process, the inventor told her husband, was now completed. Clever-Lazy had invented gunpowder.

14

Illumination

IN ORDER TO fashion containers for the fire powders, Clever-Lazy hired Not Quite and Ever Curious and, because she would not be left out, Shopshrewd. The little boys were too clumsy and fidgety to be worth the hire but Little Prune, who was growing up, proved surprisingly adept.

Not Quite was commissioned to hire more workers. Every morning girls and women from the House of Flowers came giggling and jostling into the courtyard. They sat at two long tables, laughing and chattering, gossiping and even singing as they rolled thin sheets of wood or cardboard into cylinders. Hands and fingers skilled at picking a lute string, preparing a water pipe, folding a fan, were now engaged in fashioning fragile containers from balsa wood, papier maché, cardboard. In spare moments, tiny envelopes of tissue paper were folded to hold the measured powder charges that would make the balls and rockets soar and skip.

Piled along the tabletop, they stirred and fluttered like butterflies as though already eager to take flight.

The growing piles of spheres and cylinders were stacked in barrows and taken to the limestone cave cellar. Here sat Inventor, carefully measuring and weighing the correct amounts of powder. The ratio of circumference and weight, the size and weight of the enclosed containers, the size of the firing hole all had to be taken into account. In these calculations, Clever-Lazy was helped by both Bowlmaker and Tinker, who were used to working daily with the scale and proportion of curved vessels. These two artisans also helped her to design a wide-mouthed mortar or cannon, which was to be set on a fulcrum so that the mouth could be pointed upwards to project the largest fireballs into the sky. The tinker cast three of them. They were handsome things, made of bronze.

The time finally came for the arrival of the Emperor of the Southeast. Inventor would not be called upon to take part in the ceremonies until the third day, when she was to be present at court to exhibit and explain the Imperial toys. Thereafter she would be free until the last night of the visit when she would supervise the fireworks display.

Bowlmaker insisted that Clever-Lazy be made presentable for her appearance at court. "What have you been doing to yourself?" she scolded. "You smell like a barnyard. Your hair is like straw, or is that straw sticking out of your braid? And look at those clogs! Do you spend all of your time walking through dung? You smell as though you do!"

"But I don't want to look like those girls from the House of Flowers. I have important work to do. I am an inventor!"

"You look like a pig keeper!" Bowlmaker peered closely at Tinker, too. "And *you* look like a gravedigger. Something has happened to you two. You drag around as though you were Death's best friends!"

She did not wait for an answer, but bustled off to find expert help. "I never thought I'd be asking you to take on Clever-Lazy again," she admitted as she brought Not Quite into the workshop, "but look at her!"

"At least we can get her into a good hot bath, wash her hair, clean her nails," agreed Not Quite. "Where's a big washtub?"

A few minutes later Bowlmaker returned from the courtyard shaking her head in wonder. "You'll never believe this, but someone has put a hole in the washtub. And it smells so terrible that it should be taken to the rubbish heap and burned. I'll send word to my sons to bring my own tub over here. Clever-Lazy, where's the red dress you wore to your wedding?"

But when the red dress was slipped over Clever-Lazy's head, it did not fit as it should. "I think I am fatter," said Clever-Lazy.

Not Quite and Bowlmaker glanced at one another and seemed to come to some sort of agreement about what they saw. "I think you have a child in your belly," said Not Quite.

"I think you should start taking care of yourself — and of that child," said Bowlmaker severely. Her chin shook, tears ran down her face. She put her arms around Clever-Lazy. "I'm so happy!" she said. Clever-Lazy patted her on the shoulder. She wondered what she was supposed to feel.

Scrubbed, with hair washed and braided, dressed neatly in let-out red homespun, Inventor went to court eager and curious to meet the Emperor of the Southeast, ruler of one quarter of the known world. He was a younger man than her own Emperor, Lord of the Three Quarters. His interest in the toys was keen and intelligent. He asked many questions and indicated to a scribe to take down all that was said. He was interested in the principle that made each toy perform; he was even more interested in how the toys could be used.

The owner of the toys wore his rose quartz spectacles. He listened carefully to his guest, but it was almost impossible to read his expression. He had worn the dark glasses, Clever-Lazy learned, all during the intricate negotiations concerning fishing rights, trade agreements and boundary disputes. He had also worn them when he taught his visitor to play chess. He had won three games in a row. Presumably he should be in a good humor, but now not even the dark quartz could hide the fact that he was displeased.

"The secrets of the Imperial toys," he interrupted suddenly, "should not be revealed to the vulgar."

"But have you not considered," asked the visitor politely, "that trade and commerce might be greatly improved if commoners were allowed the use of them? For instance, the wooden fish with its lodestone could be most useful to mariners. Our own ship was caught in fog; for two days the captain could not be certain of our direction. Think what a boon it would be to know where the north lies, even in fog, even on a starless night!"

Clever-Lazy, who had been listening respectfully, chimed in. "The seas themselves could be mapped and charted," she said. "There could be markings made round the edge of the saucer to help common sailors and fishermen align their course."

"Common sailors and fishermen?" asked her Emperor, the Lord of the Three Quarters. "Surely the world is going mad. It is not to our interest that every man-jack sail about the seas wherever he wants to. Better to lose a fleet of ships! Toys that give innocent pleasure to Emperors could, if shared, capsize the order of the world." He turned to the other Emperor and made a low bow. "Permit us to apologize," he said, "for the naïveté and irresponsibility of our worthless inventor."

The Emperor of the Southeast bowed in return. "O Lord of the Three Quarters," he murmured, "we bow to your superior wisdom. How wise you are! How omniscient! The world is perfect as it is."

On the last night of the visit, a great banquet was held in the palace. The pavilions were ablaze with light, the gardens lighted with the soft glow of lanterns. Tiny bells were attached to trees and bushes, even to certain flowers, to call attention to their rarity or beauty. Incense was wafted on the night air along with the scents of the garden. Musicians and dancers, jugglers and acrobats, magicians and storytellers beguiled both guests and hosts. Course after course was served and there was much wine.

Inventor and Tinker were not invited to the banquet; they would have been too excited to eat even if they had been. With the help of Bowlmaker and her seven sons, they transported the store of rockets, globes, crackers and petards from the limestone cave in a motley fleet of small boats. Under cover of twilight, they punted or rowed upstream to the foot of the palace gardens, and placed the fragile freight ashore. While Clever-Lazy, Bowlmaker and the younger sons worked to implant the rocket sticks at suitable angles, Tinker and the eldest sons made three separate trips to bring the heavy mortars, drag them up the bank and set them in place. Their wide mouths gaped at the sky.

The evening wore on. Sounds of revelry drifted through the garden to the river. Number Seven son yawned and fell asleep, his head in Bowlmaker's lap. Tinker and the eldest son sent word back that they were lying under a mulberry tree, listening to the speeches. The speeches were very long. At last Number One son came running across the garden, Tinker close at his heels. The Emperors had risen and were walking arm in arm toward the small pavilion erected for the occasion. The rustle of approaching courtiers could be heard through the trees. Suddenly they were there, all around in the darkness, settling down on lawns and hillocks like a flock of cranes. Across the river could be heard the murmurous sounds of an assembled multitude.

Expectancy hangs on the night air. There is a swish and a whine, then a sound like summer thunder. A shower of sparks bursts against the dark, explodes into another shower, climbs higher and explodes again as yet another and another rocket arcs in the sky. A murmur, a communal exultation of breath, a shout rises from both banks of the river. Emperors and commoners are equally amazed. Globes and balls climb into the air, skip and bound along the waters, reflect their own glory and make it twofold.

A dull roar thunders from the mortars; exhilarating pop-pop-pop signals the petards. The sharp tattoo of strings of firecrackers hammers at the heart. Bursting balls open like fruits or flowers to spill other balls, which release in turn fountains of cherry red and silver, green and gold, blue and white. Sparks mingle with the stars and fall hissing into the river. Still another fireball swishes upwards, opens and unfurls a flaming dragon that floats overhead.

A second dragon appears, hurling itself out of the distant sky. Great eyes blazing, it swoops down across the crowd. Part ship, part apparition, dragon ship of the Goddess, it rises suddenly, skips to the horizon and moves off toward the stars.

A great cry, almost a sob, is wrung from the crowds on either bank. Anticlimactically, a final globe explodes in midair. Fiery glyphs sprawl words of fire across the sky:

"Peace and Harmony to the two Empires." They drift like a banner, part, fade, disappear. The fireworks are over.

Silence and a nose-tingling smell hung in the darkness, then there arose a great shout from both banks. "Inventor! Inventor! Inventor!"

Clever-Lazy, flushed and streaked with powder, her hair singed, was dragged forward into the lantern light near the Emperors' pavilion. She bowed to both Emperors, then turned and bowed to the crowd thronging the shadows. Hands reached out to catch at her garments, to touch her as she passed. She was lifted up, balanced on heaving shoulders. She looked over the crowd, desperately searching for Tinker. There he was! She reached out her hands toward him, struggled to get down, disappeared with her husband into the darkness.

Dawn was ready to break when wife and husband finally reached home. Tinker fumbled for a lamp while Clever-Lazy lighted one of the phosphorous-tipped pine splinters. In a moment, the shadows were pushed back and all the dear familiarity of their workshop wrapped itself around them. A pot of soup was simmering on the brazier. They were just finishing the first bowl apiece when there came a knock on the door. They looked at each other in surprise. With a sigh Tinker rose and opened the door. The Emperor of the Southeast stood on their doorstep.

The Emperor put his finger to his lips, cautioning them not to cry out. Then, ducking his head so as not to crack it on the low frame, he stepped swiftly into the room. A brawny attendant, totally bald, followed him. The attendant closed the door behind him and stood with his back to it, arms folded over a bare chest, legs braced far apart. The Emperor's eyes glanced greedily around the workshop as though trying to devour every one of the hundreds of objects that lined shelves and rafters. He spoke to the inventor.

"My ships are anchored in the river," he said. "I found out where you live and had myself rowed over here before we cast off for good. I want to make you an offer."

The Emperor of the Southeast wanted Clever-Lazy to leave with him, to cross the sea and become his own Imperial Inventor. She would be allowed to take the tinker with her and any other items easily transportable. He glanced around the room again. "You live in a hovel! I promise you a workshop-pavilion in my court."

Tinker had been listening carefully. Now he stepped in front of Clever-Lazy, shielding her. "What is it that you really want?" he asked. He eyed the attendant at the door.

"I want to know how to make the substance that propels balls and rockets through the air," said the Emperor. "You look like a sensible man," he cajoled, "I hear you are well skilled. In my service, you would not have to work in the shadow of your wife. You will make mortars and metal balls for me and teach my generals to put them to practical purpose. Especially, I want to know how to make a dragon ship that flies through the air."

Clever-Lazy gave a low moan. Tinker glanced at her over his shoulder, signaling the merest second of shared understanding with her. "My wife and I are well-enough rewarded," he said. "We have no wish to leave here." He was aware that Clever-Lazy had stepped away from him, that she was edging back into the shadows. He thought he heard her scrape something off a shelf.

"We have no wish to use the balls and rockets for anything but toys," said Clever-Lazy. "As for the second dragon, I do not know where it came from." She was standing by the fire again, stirring soup. A small bowl of what looked like peppercorns was on the ledge next to her hand. "I decided from the very beginning that no one, not even my husband, would know how I make the firepowder. The substance is much too dangerous. I don't think you understand how much harm and suffering it could cause." She took the soup off the grate and poked the coals so that a flame leaped up.

"I think I *do* understand," returned the Emperor coolly. "It is for that very reason I must know the secret. I regret to inform you that I must take you by force." He motioned to the huge attendant. The man lunged forward, trying to bypass Tinker. Clever-Lazy slid to the right as the attendant reached to the left. She held the bowl of peppercorns, or what looked like peppercorns, clutched in one hand.

"Take cover, everybody!" she cried and tugged her husband's sleeve to emphasize her words. Next moment, bowl and contents were hurled toward the brazier. Clever-Lazy and Tinker found themselves wrapped in tight embrace under the heavy table as, with a muffled roar and a shower of sparks, the roof caved in.

15

Ruins

ASCENDING ONE WAS awakened by the explosion and thought it had gone off inside his own head. Despite his wife's warning, he had drunk far too much wine at the festival. Now, although his head floated several inches away, he was acutely aware that he could hear every animal in the barnyard. He wished he were dead.

His wife poked him and told him he must get up. Three times he tried to rise from his pallet and three times fell back. Finally, he lurched to a sitting position and allowed his wife to pull him to his feet. Leaning on her shoulder and shuddering at every step, he tottered to the window.

Smoke lingered over a hole in his inventor's roof; chunks of wood and thatch were thrown about the courtyard. Some of his servants had run into the yard, but now stood gaping at what they saw, uncertain how to proceed. Some horrid urchins, male and female, had arrived, each with a yapping dog. Ascending One reached out a hand to steady himself and turned his eyes toward Heaven. He moaned and closed his eyes, only to discover that the river scene had seared itself on his eyeballs in a reverse image of light and dark: a black sheet instead of a gold river; two large orange shapes; a blob of orange that wobbled in the foreground.

Ascending One's tongue licked at the roof of his mouth, something else licked at the back of his mind. He opened his eyes and took another look. Two ships were anchored in the river and a small boat wobbled toward them; a boat that must have come from the bottom of his garden. He wanted to tell his wife but when he opened his mouth, he became suddenly and terribly dizzy. He leaned out of the window and was sick.

Ascending One's wife took charge. She ordered the servants to enter the workshop just as Clever-Lazy and Tinker came staggering out. They were bruised and shaken and streaked with soot. Inventor's face was especially white and she was trembling so that she had to sit down. A few minutes later, she was sick; the second sick person that Ascending One's wife had had to deal with that morning. Even so, Inventor's main concern was for two men she said must still be trapped inside. She and her husband had been sheltered by the heavy worktable but there were others who had not been so protected.

The servants entered the ruins and spent half an hour lifting heavy timbers. They reported they could find no one. Only then did the smallest urchin volunteer that he had seen two men, their clothes torn, helping each other from the courtyard. One of them was bald and big, almost a giant. His arm dangled so, like a broken wing (the boy demonstrated) and his back was bleeding from a "thousand cuts." "They went that way," he said, pointing toward the river. His dog had tried to nip them.

Clever-Lazy had sat down and was listening closely. "And how about the Emp . . . I mean the other man?" she asked.

The little boy scuffed his toe in the dust. "I didn't want to look at him," he said at last.

Clever-Lazy leaned forward and said, very gently, "Tell me what you saw. My guess is that something frightened you. Tell me if I'm wrong."

A sigh escaped from the depths of the child's chest; a tear ran down his cheek. Clever-Lazy put her arms around him. "It's all right to be frightened. What did you see?"

"His face! It was all bloody. And there was something wrong with his eye." He buried his face in Clever-Lazy's shoulder, his voice muffled. "His eye wasn't where it's s'posed to be!"

Clever-Lazy turned very white. She held the small boy in her arms and rocked back and forth. Tears ran down his cheeks and tears ran down hers. After awhile, in wonder, he reached up a finger and touched the wetness of her face. "Are you frightened, too?" he asked.

"Yes, I'm frightened. And sad."

"It's all right to feel frightened," repeating the words she had said to him. "And maybe it's all right to feel sad." She smiled despite herself, and felt such a rush of love and longing that she was quite overwhelmed. She had never felt that way about a child before! The next thing she knew, he had struggled out of her arms to run across the courtyard to join his friends. She turned back to Tinker. He was watching her anxiously.

"Are you not well?" he asked.

"No. Yes! We must go to our Emperor at once and tell him what has happened. I have done something terrible!"

"You did what was right. They tried to take you away by force and you used force to prevent them. You were magnificent!"

"Magnificent? I used the firepowder in the very way I swore no one would ever use it. If I had not invented firepowder in the first place, the Emperor of the Southeast would never have been tempted. And now he's lost an eye and may be blind in the other. Aieee! I'll never be able to forgive myself."

"You acted in self-defense."

"I would rather he still had his eye." Clever-Lazy's voice was low.

"He and that big lout would have had *you*. He could make you tell him everything — the secret elements, the entire process."

"I would never tell!"

"They would torture you."

"I wouldn't tell . . ." Clever-Lazy's voice trailed off, her eyes closed. Suddenly she was asleep. I must remind you that she and Tinker had not been to bed the whole night long, and the previous day and evening had been busy and exciting. Tinker did not know yet that she was with child.

Tinker went down to the river at the bottom of the garden. The ground was confused by the activity of the night before, but there in the mud he found a pair of extremely large footprints and the fresh imprint of an unfamiliar boat. He wondered how a blind man and a man with a broken arm had managed to row themselves away. They must have been desperate. And brave.

He went back to the ruined workshop and poked about for his tools. Fortunately, he was in the habit of putting them in special order in a special place, so it was not long before he came across them. He picked up the bundle and went back to his wife. He tucked a quilt about her and lay down beside her. Soon he was asleep too.

Not until late afternoon did Ascending One seek to make an appointment with the Emperor. The Emperor, he was informed, was weary from the State visit, his head in somewhat delicate condition. He would not see anyone unless it was a matter of grave emergency, and even then not until evening.

Ascending One was faced with the difficulty of convincing the court officials that he wanted to speak about impending disaster, while at the same time concealing the fact that he had let many hours slip by without reporting either the explosion or the events leading to it. To no one, especially the Emperor of the Three Quarters, did he want to confess that he had actually seen the Emperor of the Southeast escaping from his garden. He returned home to talk to his wife.

Clever-Lazy, once awake, was eager to get to the palace. She wandered around in the wreckage looking for appropriate clothes, and finally settled for clean trousers and a quilted tunic. Tinker warned her against leaving anything valuable or dangerous for children to find. When she looked over the great jumble of her belongings, she confirmed what she already knew: nothing she owned was valuable in itself; only the relationship of one thing to another was of value. She did pick up the metal box of pine splinters and tuck it in her sleeve rather than let a child discover it and start a fire.

Looking about her, she thought of that other moment so long ago when she and her mother were leaving the bakery for the last time. Her mother had told her then to choose what she wanted most. That time she had chosen her puppets. What would she choose now? She picked up the little fish that had a piece of lodestone buried in it. She admired its cunningly-carved shape as it lay in the palm of her hand, and remembered how the Emperor of the Southeast had argued so impetuously for its extended use. Absentmindedly, she tucked the fish into the fold of her sleeve.

At twilight the Emperor gave audience to Ascending One and his inventor and the inventor's husband. He listened in astonishment to Clever-Lazy's and Tinker's story of their predawn visitors. He turned to Ascending One. Had he or any of his retainers noticed what time the visiting ships weighed anchor? Ascending One could only say, truthfully, that the ships were gone.

The Emperor was lost in thought. "Tell me again," he said. "How did the explosion occur and make a hole in your roof? I still don't understand."

Before Clever-Lazy could speak, Tinker proudly described how his wife had thrown "peppercorns that were not peppercorns" onto the flame.

"And it could cause all that damage?" asked the Emperor in amazement.

Now the inventor spoke. "The peppercorns were actually a small amount of the substance used to make the fireworks you saw at the festival, Your Highness. It would have caused much more damage if it had been confined in a ball or rocket. Fortunately, I threw just a few grains on to the fire."

"And it blew a hole through the roof?"

"That's what's so terrible. The substance could blow up a whole castle! It could destroy the wall of a city! If the secret ever gets abroad, it could be used to kill and maim vast numbers of people. It should never be used again, even as a toy."

"You are quite right," said the Emperor. "Fire powder should never again be regarded as a mere toy."

Clever-Lazy sighed in relief. "Oh, Your Highness, I knew you would understand. And now the Emperor of the Southeast must understand, too. His suffering must be terrible! Not only will he never know the secret, now he won't want to know it!"

The Emperor tapped his long curved fingernails on the carved arm of his throne. "But, *I* must have the secret," he said, "for purposes of Imperial security." Clever-Lazy began to speak, but he waved her aside and leaned forward.

"The Emperor of the Southeast will declare war on us if he lives, and if he does not, his barons will declare war in revenge." He brought the flat of his hand down hard and struck the chair arm. *"We must strike them before they strike us!"*

He turned to Ascending One. "Tomorrow hire as many workers as you need and set Inventor to direct the process of manufacture. All of you will be handsomely rewarded." He cast a shrewd eye on Ascending One. "For you there will be titles, prestige, perhaps nobility if you do the job well and quickly." He turned to Inventor and her husband. "For you –"

"I will not be bought!" declared Clever-Lazy. Her eyes flashed. "I will take no part in the making of fire powder nor tell what it's made of!" The Emperor gazed at her in astonishment. There was a low moan from Ascending One. Tinker reached out and took her hand.

Inventor and her husband were thrown into a cell in the deepest, darkest dungeon. Tinker's tools, which he had brought to the palace with him, were confiscated by the guards, but the box of pine splinters and the little fish that Clever-Lazy carried in her sleeve were ignored.

The two of them lay on a pile of moldy straw and talked and dozed long hours away. "I should have known from the very beginning," Clever-Lazy berated herself. "For months, I dealt in dirt and dung, bones and ashes – everything that is finished, used up, dead. Oh, Tinker, wouldn't it be terrible if the soldiers who died on the battlefield should be the means to kill thousands and thousands more?" She had crept into Tinker's arms and curled herself into a ball to be comforted.

Tinker patted her shoulder and held her close while she wept. He told her of the vision he had had when digging dirt from the battlefield. "How did you keep yourself from telling me?" asked Clever-Lazy, sitting up, peering at him in the dark.

"I told myself there wasn't time. I told myself we must keep our promise to Ascending One. I wanted so much for us to have what I did not have as a child, Clever-Lazy. I thought that your parents would have been pleased and in that way, I would be respectable. I should have paid attention to myself when I said I felt corrupted."

"*I* should have paid attention when I first signed the contract with Ascending One," said Clever-Lazy. "To sell one's mind is as bad as to sell one's body. Maybe worse. I've been in such a frenzy that I've not thought about my parents. And I had almost forgotten about the Goddess."

She sat up suddenly. "Tinker, was it only last night that we displayed the fireworks?" She did not wait for an answer. "I remember now that something happened, something I did not expect. There was a dragon . . ."

"Yes, and it was spectacular. How ever did you manage it, Clever-Lazy?"

"But there were two dragons. One of them I fashioned myself from wire and whalebone that floated free when a fireball opened. The second dragon I had nothing to do with. It was the dragon ship of the Goddess."

"Perhaps we only imagine that we saw two dragons, Clever-Lazy. Much has happened in the last twenty-four hours. Our memories are playing tricks on us."

"But we both remember. And the Emperor of the Southeast remembered the same thing. He called it a dragon ship."

"Clever-Lazy, we are in mortal danger. It is better to believe that there is no Goddess."

Sometime, in the long night, Ascending One came to visit them. He was much frightened, both on his own account and theirs. "You have ruined me," he wailed. He begged Clever-Lazy to give in gracefully. "There is still a chance to win our way back into the favor of the Emperor, Clever-Lazy. But you must act quickly, before they wring the secret from you. I warn you, they will use torture."

Tinker listened gravely. Clever-Lazy reached out and touched his hand. "Don't worry so! They dare not kill me lest they lose the secret." Tinker and Ascending One exchanged a long look. Both of them sighed.

Ascending One volunteered new information. "The Emperor is in consultation with his astrologers. What happens to you and how fast it happens may depend on them. There have been strange portents." As though afraid he had said too much, he called the guards and departed.

Again Clever-Lazy and Tinker were left in darkness. When morning came they had no way of knowing. The hours dragged on. Once or twice a guard peered in at them, staring down at them silently while he raised his torch. Another guard brought them sour rice and a pitcher of stale water. Clever-Lazy slept most of the time, but the tinker lay in darkness with his eyes open. Of the two, it is difficult to say which was the braver. Clever-Lazy denied the very possibility of death and torture, and put faith in the Goddess. Tinker thought of it most of the time and was afraid for his wife.

Sometime, during the second day, Clever-Lazy told him about the baby.

16

The Tax Collector

TINKER TOLD HIMSELF that he could not believe he was going to be a father, but if he were not, whence came this surge of joy? Then he remembered that he and Clever-Lazy lay in a dungeon, and that they might both be hauled out of their cell to be tortured or killed without a moment's warning. A gloom blacker than any prison gloom descended upon his mind and heart. Gloom was followed by anger. He found himself shouting at Clever-Lazy.

How could she, he asked, not tell him this most important of all news? Only then did he lower his voice. How could she risk her life if she knew another life depended on it? It was all very well to be concerned for thousands of faceless others, born and unborn, but how could she fail to care most for their own child?

Clever-Lazy clawed through her mind, confused and overwhelmed. She tried to tell Tinker how it was that

Bowlmaker and Not Quite had made her aware that she might be bearing a child. She had been too busy to pay much attention, but since then she had noticed that she was more sleepy than usual and sometimes dizzy in the mornings, and these observations had just begun to convince her that the older women may have been right. As for the long weeks and months before, when she was working day and night to prepare the fireworks, she had lost count of time and had paid little attention to herself. She had been so intent on being clever that she had forgotten to be lazy.

She remembered the kingfisher on the battlefield and the few hours she and Tinker had spent dozing and talking there. Perhaps that was when they had started their baby. And she wanted to tell Tinker about the moment when she had held the small boy in her arms, and he had told her it was all right to be sad. Then she had felt a strange rush of joy. Was this what it was like, being a mother? Tinker was so angry she was afraid he might dismiss the incident. Perhaps she had better become accustomed to the feeling, let it grow a little, before sharing it with anyone — even Tinker.

The hours dragged on. Tinker wanted to call the guards to tell them the whole thing was a mistake, that his wife had changed her mind, would tell all. The only flaw in the plan was that Clever-Lazy had *not* changed her mind. He was afraid that the guards would come, and that his action would release a chain of events that would lead even more quickly to disaster.

Husband and wife kept to separate corners of the cell, each hunched and brooding. Tinker's thoughts dwelt on how stubborn Clever-Lazy was, with every now and then an unwelcome and irrational feeling of love and tenderness toward her and their baby. Clever-Lazy felt hurt and bewildered. She thought of her mother and wished she were alive. Thinking of her mother made her think of the Goddess.

Noises in the corridor! Tinker stood up and peered through the bars as the flicker of torches approached. An official in court dress appeared out of the shadows, accompanied by guards. Clever-Lazy stared at him dully, the tinker warily. "Inventor, I have come to question you about nonpayment of taxes," said the man, and sat himself on a little stool. He motioned one of the guards to fix a torch in the wall sconce, then dismissed them all. He waited while their footsteps and hoarse voices dwindled to confused echoes down the corridor.

"Clever-Lazy?" asked the man. She turned her head. "Clever-Lazy, attached to the patronage of the honorable Ascending One?" She nodded. The man paused as though deciding how to proceed. "Clever-Lazy, daughter of Baker and Baker's husband who lived in the Province of Dancing Mountains?" She gave a little start. The man hurried on. "Inventor of saffron buns, cleaner of ovens, puppeteer extraordinary? Inventor of the abacus?"

Clever-Lazy leaned forward in the darkness, peered into the man's face. "Could you be . . . are you . . . ? You *are* the tax collector!"

"Shhh! Pretend you don't know me," he whispered. He turned to Tinker, ignoring his scowl. "I've ordered the guards to let me talk to you in private. They are not apt to be suspicious since I often come here to question debtors. When there is no better reason to throw someone into the dungeon, the Emperor often orders me to find some flaw in the matter of taxes. I do so as the Minister of the Imperial Treasure."

"How is it that I have never seen you at court?" asked Clever-Lazy.

"Partly because I didn't want to upset Ascending One. He has a habit of fearing the worst from me and would interpret our friendship as a threat. He has never forgiven me, you know, for being appointed to the office he aspired to." The tax collector sighed. "Often and often, Clever-Lazy, I wish I had never asked you for your abacus that day."

"But it brought you an important and respectable position," Tinker interjected. "Clever-Lazy has told me the story, and I have heard Ascending One complain how you introduced the use of the abacus to the Emperor. How did you manage to hide yourself so?"

"My job does not entail being popular, so there is no special reason to show myself. By nature I am retiring. Besides, my wife was ill. When I was not consulting with the Emperor or attending meetings or at work in the counting house, I spent the time in our pavilion trying to be a comfort to my wife."

"Where is she now?" asked Clever-Lazy.

"She died two weeks ago." He looked from Clever-Lazy to her husband. "I imagine you two, above all others, can understand how much I miss her. We loved each other dearly."

Clever-Lazy and Tinker shifted a little uneasily, stole a glance at one another. "We understand," said Tinker. His voice was gruff. Clever-Lazy touched the tax collector's hand through the bars. "Tell me about her," she said.

A tear ran down Tax Collector's cheek. He wiped it away unashamedly. "I don't have many people here at court who ask about her. She came from a village not far from yours, Clever-Lazy." He hesitated, choosing his words carefully. "She knew . . . she knew who your mother was. She believed . . . but it is not wise to say what she believed. She was all alone and she told me more than she otherwise might have. You must remember that she knew she was dying.

"My wife was happy in her own province. When we came to live at court, she withered before my eyes. The other women made fun of her big feet, her country speech, her superstitions. They thought she didn't see or under-stand their mockery, but she was smarter than they knew.

"I wanted to give up my position, but the Emperor would not grant me permission. In his own way he is a shrewd man, the Emperor. He would not let me resign even though I argued that Ascending One is more clever and eager than I. He contended that Ascending One would never know when he had reached the top, that he would always reach for more. Better to keep him on a lower rung! So that is how I was kept from leaving the court even though my wife was dying.

"Then *you* appeared at court, Clever-Lazy. My wife was so excited when she realized you were the baker's child. The women of the province had feared that both of you had died and with you, certain ancient knowledge . . . Well, no matter. She was not a gossip, but she collected every shred of news about you and your accomplishments, your way of life, your happiness with your husband. She was certain, however, that one day you would need help. She believed it was an omen that our paths had crossed. She made me promise that when she died, I would watch over you."

Tax Collector paused. The thought of his dying wife had made sadness drift across his round good-humored face as a cloud drifts across the moon. He gave himself a little shake. "So," he said, holding out his arms and indicating the gloom that surrounded them, "so here I am!"

"So here *we* are," amended Tinker bitterly. "Now what are we going to do?"

Clever-Lazy spoke from the shadows. "If we could get out of this prison, we could run away to —"

"Do not tell me where you would run," interrupted Tax Collector. "It is best I don't know. For I do have a plan. It is quite simple, actually. Tonight I shall return —"

"Tonight?" asked Clever-Lazy.

"Is it not night now?" queried Tinker.

"No, it's high noon. You've lost all count of time, I see. You do not really control the heavens."

"What do you mean by that?" asked Tinker.

"The astrologers say that you released a dragon who gave birth to a bigger dragon. They say that you are in league with the Emperor of the Southeast to steal our moon, but due to the wisdom of our Emperor and the suspicions of Ascending One, you were caught in the nick of time. The whole city is in a turmoil."

"That's ridiculous," sputtered Clever-Lazy. "The dragon was just a toy made of wire and whalebone, and made an outline of a dragon flutter in the night sky until it burned out."

"And the dragon ship?" asked Tinker.

"I don't know where it came from."

"Then tell that to the Emperor," Tinker pleaded. "Get back in his good graces, Clever-Lazy! Or we will be executed for sure."

Clever-Lazy grimaced. "I don't believe the Emperor is interested in the dragon ship. What he wants is the secret of the firepowder, so he can win a war against the Southeast. His astrologers are telling lies and tales as part of a campaign to whip up the people."

"Clever-Lazy," said Tax Collector gently, "if the Emperor cannot get the secret any other way, he will torture you."

She smiled at him. "Ah," she said, "but you have come to help us escape. What is your plan, dear old friend?"

"One of the oldest in the world," said Tax Collector. "I never was a very original fellow." His voice became more serious. "As I leave this time, Tinker, I shall officially seize your valuable tools toward payment of taxes. I shall smuggle them in under my robes when I return, and you can pick the lock. I shall keep talking and clicking my abacus while you make your way out of the dungeon. I do talk a lot, you know. The guards have long since stopped listening."

"How will we find our way through the corridors?" asked Clever-Lazy.

"I have a map for you to study," said Tax Collector and touched his sleeve. He waved the map triumphantly as he brought it forth. "You see, I have thought of everything."

"But you haven't thought about what's going to happen when they find we are gone," growled Tinker.

Tax Collector clapped a hand to his brow. "Dear me! So I haven't! If my wife were here, she'd tell me how absent-minded I've become."

"If your wife were here, she would say you are very brave," said Clever-Lazy tenderly. "We must think of another plan."

"Clever-Lazy!" Tinker's voice was grim. "Tax Collector's offer is the best we'll ever have. We must get away! You have not only yourself to think of, but our baby as well. If you are held here, they will torture you and get the secret from you. If you escape, you will save not only our child but generations of other children."

Tax Collector's round face lighted up with joy. "Oh, if only my wife could hear the news! It's like having our own grandchild." His manner sobered abruptly. "Clever-Lazy, take your child and take your secret to some safe place. I'm an old man left all alone. I don't want to die, but I don't want to live if something happens to you. Surely it would be the wish of my wife that I help you save yourself. If my wife were here, she would tell you that this is the best thing I have ever done."

"Tax Collector, I cannot bear it! I am afraid of what may happen to you. Surely you are the bravest man who ever lived."

"Then you must be brave, too, Clever-Lazy — brave enough to receive what I choose to give."

Tinker's voice was harsh with emotion. "We shall never forget you, Tax Collector, and we shall make sure our child will hear the story of what you have done."

"This is a happy day, my first in a long time." Then he stood up. "Time to call the guards. Tinker, I shall bring your tools so you can pick the lock and take them with you on your journey. Clever-Lazy, what can I bring that will be of use to you?"

Clever-Lazy touched the little wooden fish in her sleeve and felt the outline of the flat tin box containing the pine splinters. "I have what I need most," she said.

17

Following the Fish

WHEN CLEVER-LAZY AND Tinker emerged from the dungeon keep, they found the streets alive with people. Men, women and children were running about in the darkness, shouting, beating gongs and pans, dancing to the beat of drums. They joined a long line of dancers who were being led in single file by a figure who bobbed and menaced in an elaborate dragon mask. The two escaped prisoners danced with heads down, hoping no one would recognize them in a sudden flare of torch light.

When they reached one of the city gates, Tinker signaled to Clever-Lazy to break off from the line and follow him. Together they slipped through the gate. Once outside the city walls, they found themselves in humid darkness. The air, close and still, gave hint of a subdued storm. Tinker said they had come out of the East Gate. The Dancing Mountains lay far to the north and west. Tinker had many doubts about trying to reach the Dancing Mountains.

"The first place the Emperor's soldiers will look," he argued, "is the river route and the roads that lead to your home village. Often I have traveled there, stopping off at every house. I am too well-known. Coming downstream I take passage on the riverboat. Every captain and crewman knows me; probably many of my customers will be among the passengers. No, we can't go that way."

Clever-Lazy was determined to go to the Dancing Mountains and she had an alternate plan for getting there. "Go east!" she said. "We can head east for several days before we turn north and cut to the northwest. The Emperor's men will be thoroughly confused."

"It's we who will be confused. A few yards from the gate and we lose direction in the darkness. Once we leave the road, we'll wander in circles. And if we stay on the road, they'll catch us in no time."

Clever-Lazy felt in the fold of her sleeve. "Tinker," she asked, "do you carry a rice bowl in your pack? We can fill it with water from the ditch and set my little wooden fish afloat. The fish always knows where the north star is even if we don't. We can be certain that we are going east by always going to the needle's right. As long as we are headed east, the fish will point to my left hand."

Since there was nothing else to do, Tinker allowed himself to be persuaded to scramble across the ditch, pausing only to dip some water in his rice bowl. The two of them huddled behind a stone while Clever-Lazy struck one of the pine splinters to make a light. Then, she placed the lodestone fish on the surface of the water. The fish swung around slowly, then settled in one direction.

"The soldiers will not expect us to be able to travel quickly on a starless night," mused Tinker, then paused, surprised by the enthusiasm that had crept into his voice. "Well, we'll try it your way, Clever-Lazy. I have no better plan. But we must hurry! Our advantage lies in speed. We must cut through the zones nearest the city before they expect us to. We might be just lucky enough to get through." His voice became sober again. "But remember, Clever-Lazy, that's when our real journey begins. It may take us months to reach the Dancing Mountains. Some-how, before winter comes, we must travel almost a thou-sand miles."

For hours they traveled in darkness, slipping and stum-bling on the muddy banks of the ditch, which gave them added guidance. However, when the ditch curved to the south, they followed and did not realize their error until they took time out to light a pine splint and take their bearings. They doused the light and headed east again with much less certainty. They stopped so often and used up splints at such an alarming rate that Clever-Lazy searched through Tinker's pack to find a candle. She floated it in the bowl along with the fish. Their improvised binnacle made a tiny will-o-the-wisp that flickered faintly as they carried it along.

Resolutely they kept going east, striking out across fields, splashing through rice paddies. When dawn broke, they found themselves near a small green hill that stuck up like an island in the watery landscape. A sort of path or terrace wound itself around the hill, a white spiral that seemed to serve no particular purpose but glistened in the gray dawn.

They splashed their way to the hill and hauled themselves up to the first level. Rather than follow the spiral, they clambered directly to the summit where a tuft of trees offered meager shelter. Part of the hill had fallen inward, taking a few trees with it, and exposing several large stone blocks. They crept into a cleft between the rocks, which was filled with a debris of decayed cedar and tumbled smaller rocks, and curled themselves into a ball behind a screen of dead branches. When the sun rose, they checked their direction and, with a sigh of exhaustion and relief, fell asleep in each other's arms.

They awoke in the afternoon and lay in their hiding place, looking out across the inundated fields. They watched some women wading in the rice paddies, harvesting grain. Clever-Lazy scrounged some mushrooms that grew from an old stump near the cleft, and Tinker was able to crawl down the hill for water. At sunset, the villagers left the fields. When the shadows were long, Tinker edged his way to the nearest crops and gathered green rice. The kernels were sweet and milky, easy to chew. Even the tender green shoots gave good nourishment. They stored more rice in Tinker's pack. "We are lucky to be traveling in harvest season," said Clever-Lazy.

"Winter follows harvest," Tinker reminded her.

By daylight, they had noticed a narrow dike aligned to the east. Most dikes were curved and short, their length decided by ancient farm boundaries and the contour of the land, but this one went straight. When night came, they followed the dike, never deviating and cutting across all obstacles. As long as they walked carefully, one foot in front of the other, there was no need for the binnacle.

At last the path came to an end. They struck a light and took a bearing, with the aid of the fish. Clever-Lazy begged for a rest even though Tinker warned her that dawn was approaching. She leaned her cheek against the cool stone. Where she had expected smoothness, there were lines cut deep into the rock. She traced them with her finger; a spiral was carved snakelike the length of the stone.

Urged on by her husband, she rose and stumbled forward. She had not known she was so tired! Although it was still dark, dawn was coming as they scrambled up an abrupt rise. A stone pillar was silhouetted against the graying sky. She looked downhill, trying to see the stone she had rested against at the end of the dike. The two stones — the stone where she had rested and the stone where she now stood — were in alignment. Painfully she pulled herself up the hill, sometimes using her hands to grasp roots and stones as the grade steepened. As often as possible, she lifted her eyes to the upright stone at the top of the terraced hillside. At last, she reached the standing stone and leaned against one side while Tinker leaned against the other. They stood on the overhang of a cliff. Clever-Lazy reached out, her fingers searching for the long carved snake. At first, she was disappointed, then she found a carved disk. Within the disk was a spiral.

Tinker decided that they should go forward, over the cliff. Certainly they could not stay where they were! He began to pick his way down the escarpment, whispering encouragement to Clever-Lazy to follow closely. The cliff was of limestone with many ridges and small nesting holes where swifts and owls sheltered. It was easy to find foothold even though the drop was steep. Nevertheless, Tinker worried that if dawn should break before they were down, they would be caught like flies on a wall. In the morning mist, he could begin to see miles of countryside laid out below where hardly a rabbit could move without being marked. Would they be better off once they were down the cliff? Perhaps they could find shelter behind the giant boulders that were strewn at the base.

Tinker looked up to see Clever-Lazy's feet above him, and let himself down another notch while he searched for a foothold for himself below. His foot touched nothing, although he swung it wide from side to side. His eyes, so accustomed to darkness, could see well in the predawn. He looked up beyond Clever-Lazy and saw the boulder at the edge of the cliff, foreshortened and seeming to bend over to watch him; he looked down and saw a ridge, a slightly jutting lip, below. He closed his eyes.

"If I were Clever-Lazy, I would pray to the Goddess," he

said to himself. He had time only for a brief grim smile, then let himself drop. Next moment he found himself staring into the mouth of a cave. The opening was concealed from above by the overhanging angle of the cliff, from below by the upthrust ledge he was standing on. He called soft encouragement to his wife, and stood by to catch her as she dropped the last few feet. They crept into the cave just as the sun gilded the flooded terraces to the east.

In the late afternoon they awoke to the sound of a horse's whinny, the stamping of a hoof, the jingle of harness. Above them, from the top of the cliff, they could hear voices. Tinker crept forward, trying to catch a few words. In a few minutes Clever-Lazy tugged at his jacket, signaling him to turn. Her finger was at her lips and she motioned to the back of the cave, then upward. When he still failed to catch her meaning, she pulled at her ear and pointed to the roof of the cave again. Quiet as a snake, she slithered along the rock floor. Tinker followed. By some trick of rock formation, the sound at the top of the cliff was perfectly audible from the back of the cave.

"Is this as far as we come?" The voice was male, probably a very young man or an older boy.

The voice that answered was gruffer, harsher. "I don't care what the captain says. They couldn't have come this far without being picked up by one of the patrols."

"Unless they traveled at night," returned the younger voice.

"Nothing's been able to move the last few nights. With the roads barricaded, no one could get through."

"What if they didn't go by road?"

"How many times do I have to say it? They'd get lost before they ever came this far. No, they're holed up in the city somewhere. Or gone off with the Southies' Emperor."

"What do you think, Scar? Do you think the woman's really a sorceress? They say she digs up cadavers from old graveyards and makes them do her bidding."

"People say a lot of things. And who gets sent to check them out? Some idiot farmer reported he saw a light floating along between Heaven and earth last night. A friend of mine was ordered out to splash around the rice paddies until dawn. Says he was a farmer's son himself, and knows that sometimes bubbles of gas rise in the rice paddies. On thunderous nights, they light up and flicker in the dark."

"Even I know that, Scar."

"Think you're so smart? You'd probably still be splashing around in the wet. My friend's no raw recruit. He found that farmer's hut and made himself snug with the farmer's wife the rest of the night. That'll teach 'em."

"Do you think people really saw a dragon ship?"

"I saw it, you fool. I was on guard at the palace that night. Saw it with my own eyes — and my scar's been itchin' ever since."

"So why couldn't she and her husband just . . . well, fly away? Disappear? She could probably whistle for a dragon easy as you could for a sedan chair."

"Easier, on the pay I get! Well, we'd better get to work. Captain says this countryside is riddled with caves, and

that one of them around here is called Dragon's Hole. I'll
lower you over the cliffside and you can tell me if you see
anything."

"Not me, you don't. I'm not crawling into a dragon's sty.
What if I *did* find the sorceress — or a dragon? I don't care
what reward they give me."

"Reward? Soldiers don't get rewards. We just do what
we're told. Captain told us to go to the edge of the cliff."

"Just to the edge? No farther?"

"Sometimes you're not so dumb, Bumpkin. C'mon. One
of the first things you learn in the army is never go farther
than you're told."

18

Dragon Lines

THE JINGLE OF harness departed in the distance, but Clever-Lazy and Tinker continued to lie in cramped positions for a long time. They dared not make a sound for fear they could be heard above ground as easily as they had heard voices below. At length, Clever-Lazy rolled over on her back, rubbing a sore elbow, while Tinker explored toward the rear of the cave. It lay in deep shadow with almost no light from the entrance.

"Find anything?" she asked.

"No. Just the place where the ceiling arcs down to the floor. Sometimes limestone caves go for miles under the earth, but not this one. My grandfather used to warn me about caves. He told me to use them for shelter if I had no other choice, but to always stay near the entrance. He was afraid of evil spirits."

"I wonder if this cave is the one they call Dragon's

Hole," said Clever-Lazy suddenly interested. She crawled back into the shadows with Tinker and felt carefully with her fingertips along the rough walls. She was not entirely surprised to discover a disk enclosing a spiral cut into the rock. Satisfied, she returned with Tinker to the mouth of the cave. Together they sat and watched the darkening sky.

Tinker looked out from the cave and saw dark clouds gathering over the landscape. 'No moon again tonight,' he thought. The shadow of the cliff dominated the near view but directly east, beyond the shadow, the ruins of a little temple reflected the ruddy sunset. Tinker noticed that as it ran northward, the escarpment slanted into the ground, and let enough light from the sun spill over so that each landmark cast its own separate shadow. He wondered anxiously what they would do when they could no longer follow the shelter of the cliff.

Clever-Lazy did see and did not see the same thing as Tinker. As if in a vision, she saw every isolated tree and stone and mound on a great plain that stretched uninterrupted northward. The lonely landmarks seemed to her to be arranged along the spokes and laterals of a giant cobweb laid out just under the surface of the earth. A vibrant current, barely discernible, coursed through the network. '*The earth is alive,*' she exclaimed to herself, and felt a wave of exultation. '*Earth is alive and Heaven is alive and somehow they draw strength from one another!*'

She turned to her husband. "Tinker, we don't need the fish any more! There's a way to follow lines in the earth, to feel the current in our own bodies just as the fish feels the pull of the north star. There is a current that we can ride just as a leaf floats along on a river." When Tinker shook his head in bewilderment, she refused to believe that he could not see what she saw. "Look! Look!" But for all her pointing and explaining, the tinker could not, would not, see.

Together they discussed their plans while they sat and waited for the darkness. Clever-Lazy wanted to leave the shelter of the cliff and venture out into the landscape to the nearest hill. From there, they could align themselves with the next landmark and follow the lines. "Tinker, I think the lines, the force in the lines, will lead us directly to the shrine of the Goddess."

Tinker was at first scornful, then angry. "Clever-Lazy, you don't seem to understand that we and our child are in great danger. Our one chance is to take no chances. We must go northward as swiftly and surely as possible. The way to do that is to stay close to the cliff as long as we can."

"Listen to me. The swiftest and surest way is to follow the lines."

"What lines? I've tried and tried, Clever-Lazy, but I don't see any paths out there."

"I'm not talking about roads or paths. I'm talking about something *in* the earth, not on it. Something under the earth's skin, something shining, like a cobweb. The earth is filled with power. I saw it! Instead of using the power, we are fighting and struggling against it."

Still Tinker shook his head. His plan was to follow the escarpment, keeping it on their left as they wended their way among the boulders and shale fallen at its base. He would go down the cliff first. He stepped over the sill of the natural porch that screened the entrance to the cave, and began to edge his way down the limestone facing. Clever-Lazy soon lost sight of him in the darkness, although she could hear the faint scraping noise of his progress.

Clever-Lazy gazed outward to the night-obscured horizon, trying to adjust her eyes to the murk. 'I can hardly see my hand before my face,' she thought. A streak of light shot across the sky from north to south.

Clever-Lazy blinked and shook her head. There it was again! A globe of light skipped to the obscured horizon directly east, paused for a moment to illuminate the ruins of the little temple, then came rushing toward her. *Closer, the globe seemed to be an enormous head, mouth agape, eyes shining, claws extended from its foreshortened body. Silently it swooped almost to the mouth of the cave. Just as she was about to cry out in terror, it bounded straight upward and over the top of the cliff.*

"Tinker!"

"Shhh! I'm right here. Don't make so much noise." Tinker's head appeared on the ledge, then he pulled himself up and over. "The climb's not so bad. Once you get started, there are footholds and handholds, almost like a ladder. I reached bottom much faster and easier than I thought I would."

"Tinker, I saw a dragon. Didn't you see it, too?"

"Of course, I didn't. For one thing, I had my nose pressed against the cliff."

"But didn't you see the light? It must have flashed on the cliff when it was coming on a level, before it rose up toward the stone up there."

"I saw a reflection when the moon broke through, if that's what you mean. It was gone almost as soon as it came." Exasperation edged Tinker's voice. "Clever-Lazy, I don't know what is happening to you."

"I think like I think," returned Clever-Lazy icily. "And I saw a dragon."

Night after night they made their way along the base of the escarpment. During the day, they crept into a crack in the cliff or slept under the shelter of one of the fallen boulders. As they progressed northward, the countryside became less inhabited so they occasionally took a chance and made their way in late afternoon shadow or twilight, flitting from one rocky hiding place to another. Still, the nights were cloudy and the moon rarely showed itself. They lost all count of time.

Tinker was worried. If they turned west too soon, they might wander into an area patrolled by the Emperor's soldiers. On the other hand, to continue north indefinitely might lead them into a maze of mountain ranges where they could become lost and cut off from the shrine of the Goddess. The harvest season was at its height, but soon it would wane; autumn would come and snow would fall in the high passes. To make matters worse, the cliff, that for so many miles had acted as hiding place and guide, had dwindled to a mere rocky fault that would soon disappear into the ground. But Clever-Lazy refused to worry.

The time came when Tinker could no longer claim that the cliff offered shelter or hiding place. Despite his grumbling, Clever-Lazy persuaded him to abandon all that was left of it, and to move out to a pile of stones that lay to the northwest. As they approached, a small herd of sheep shied away and ran bleating through one of the gaps in the rough circle of stones. Tinker argued that the stones were nothing but part of a crude enclosure for livestock. The stones were certainly unremarkable, low boulders no doubt lugged from the escarpment, and set widely apart to make the circle. Two taller stones marked what might have been a gate.

They decided to spend the night there and lay down by the stone in the center, which had seemed to attract the sheep. When they awoke at dawn, they found the sheep had returned and were huddled about them. Clever-Lazy leaped up to shoo them away, and then took the opportunity to walk all around the circle, ever aware of her husband's watchful eye. Finally she went back to the stone in the center and sat down in the lowest part of it.

The stone proved to be surprisingly comfortable, almost like a hollowed-out chair. She let her hands caress the "arms" slightly raised on either side of her, and became aware that the fingertips of her left hand had discovered a carved groove. She recognized the familiar disk, the spiral.

Tinker had wandered off to inspect the stone circle and now was standing, blocking her view through the two taller stones that marked the gate. He returned to where she was sitting in her stone chair. At her insistence, he knelt to trace the carved symbol. She found herself able to sight between the tall gate stones much as though she was looking through the cross hairs of a soldier's bow. She saw a low hill several miles away, notched on one side. Through the slight depression, she saw the peak of another hill, almost a mountain, looming in the clear air many miles distant. On its flank, cut out from the turf and glistening with white chalk, was the outline of a dragon.

For days they struggled across the landscape like two ants progressing from one hill or cairn to another. Clever-Lazy had hoped that the dragon lines would bear them effortlessly, but no such miracle occurred. One foot in front of the other was all that carried them forward and the terrain was not easy. Unlike a road, the lines went straight from one point to another, up forbidding embankments, down steep hillsides, across intervening waterways. They were forced to detour often, and used the lodestone fish to get back in alignment again. Decisions had to be made, arguments ensued, and Tinker had to be persuaded.

The hill they had seen through the stone viewfinder proved not to be a prelude to the foothills of the Dancing Mountains, as they had hoped, but stood solitary on the plain. Instead of gaining altitude, the terrain sloped gradually downward and the ground, which had been for so many miles hard and rocky, now turned soft and muddy. They were entering a vast marsh of unexpected pools of black water, creeping trickles of green water and squishy mool, which squirted when they stepped on them. Mist hung everywhere.

They floundered for a full day and when night came, they were glad to lay themselves down in the hollow of a huge fallen tree. Its black roots trailed in the water, but the silvery trunk, partly filled with wood rot, made a relatively dry and soft sleeping place. In the morning, they each caught a fish and built themselves the first fire of the entire journey to cook their catch.

Warmed and satisfied, they snuggled down in the log to discuss what their next move should be. Tinker wanted to leave Clever-Lazy to rest while he cast about for a trail to take them through the bog. Clever-Lazy did not want to separate from him for fear he would become lost from her. "Better to be lost together," she argued, "than to be splashing about looking for each other."

"We're lost now, Clever-Lazy," he responded, "and I'm afraid we've wasted too much time following your . . . your cobweb. So now we've caught ourselves in it! We'll be lucky if we get to our destination before the snow cuts us off. And once we get there, what shall we do? How shall we keep warm? What shall we eat? Don't forget we have a baby to fend for."

"The baby won't be born until the end of winter, almost into spring. And don't *you* forget that we are under the protection of the Goddess. She'll look after us. I don't mean that she will make life easy, but I know we will survive. Besides, where else can we go?"

Tinker stood up and started to stow their belongings into his pack. He tried to keep his voice even, not wanting to quarrel. "I don't have as much faith in the Goddess as you do, Clever-Lazy. Sometimes I wonder if she exists at all."

"How can you say such a dreadful thing!" exclaimed Clever-Lazy. She was on her feet, eyes blazing. "The Goddess has protected our family since the beginning of time. Once she had temples and priestesses all over Earth. Perhaps she could fly from one to the other in her dragon ship. My mother, her grandmother —" she stopped, her voice choked with outrage.

Tinker was maddeningly calm. "I've heard your stories before, Clever-Lazy," he said. "Now you listen to me. I'm going to leave you here for a little while, and go find a path that will lead us out of this swamp. Whatever you do, don't leave the log. I'll take my bearings from here."

Tinker splashed off determinedly, but almost as soon as he was out of sight, he found that it was impossible to go in a straight line. Within a few minutes, he had come to a pool too deep to cross and had to edge around it. Once on the other side, he made progress for awhile by leaping from one tussock to another. When he came to an old stone causeway, obviously man-made, his hopes rose high. But the causeway led him to deeper water again, where a tangle of old tree trunks and stunted snags rose like gravestones above the surface. He realized that he was looking at a submerged forest, and when the causeway came to an end and was itself submerged, he decided to turn back to find Clever-Lazy. Mist had closed in behind him and a steady rain was pocking the waters.

Meanwhile Clever-Lazy, still smarting from Tinker's confession of disbelief, sat and fumed in the silver-barked log. If only she had persuaded him to let her look for higher ground! She had told him she was sure there was a hill from which they could get a new alignment. How had she allowed herself to promise to stay by this stupid log? From here, she could see little but mist and brambles. Worse, the mist was changing to rain.

At least she could do something to protect herself! Clever-Lazy jumped out of the log, which already was rocking in a brown puddle, and tore at the ropelike vines that covered one end of it. She placed dead sticks across the hollow as small supporting beams, interwove them clumsily with the vines, and shingled her new roof with whatever came to hand: smoothed-out scrolls of bark, armfuls of reeds, heaps of dried leaves and a plaster of mud. She was not an inventor for nothing.

Cross and tired, wet with rain and mud, yet proud of her handiwork, Clever-Lazy crawled into the dark cocoon she had constructed for herself. She lay in the hollow of the log, listened to the rain, revelled in the surprising warmth and snugness, and felt herself being gently rocked and soothed. Soon she was asleep.

Outside the puddle overflowed into the larger pool; the gnarled roots yielded to insistent coaxing; and the log, which had been held in large part by the thicket of vines now used for the roof, floated out into deeper water. The rain fell, the waters rose and the silver-hulled vessel was borne away on an ever-swiftening current.

19

The Buried Moon

TINKER NOTED WITH dismay the rapid rise of waters. He must go back and find Clever-Lazy before the causeway was covered. He began to run, but fast as he ran, he still had to swim for higher ground. He was a good swimmer and knew how to tie his pack on his head so as not to lose it. He hauled himself up on a steep bank and was lying there gasping, when he heard the sound of men's voices. He climbed up the slope and saw a clearing. Soldiers were setting up a dome-shaped yurt, cursing and complaining as they struggled in the mud. The clearing was the top of a small hill, a flattened cone similar to the landmarks he and his wife had used in their travels. Clever-Lazy had been convinced that such a hill existed in the marsh, but he had been too angry to pay attention.

More men entered the clearing, first their heads and then the rest of their bodies appeared as they topped the opposite rise. Horses were dragged up the incline. More shouting, the sound of something big crashing in the underbrush, and an elephant made its way over the brow of the hill. Cooking fires smoked and steamed in the rain.

Tinker realized he was in danger. Any moment, men would come to search his side of the hill for firewood or shelter. He wriggled back into the bushes and looked down at the water swirling below. By this time the hill was probably an island. How could he find his wife in a landscape that changed its contours moment by moment?

Two men had crossed the clearing and were descending the hillside close by. They were so stealthy in their movements that at first he thought they had come to ambush him, then he decided they were only two soldiers bent on shunning their duties. Their voices sounded familiar, although Tinker could not remember having seen them before. The taller one was hardly more than a gangling boy. The other was heavyset, paunchy. When the older man turned his head to look about, which he did often, he revealed a deep scar, which ran down the side of his nose to furrow his cheek. It was not, Tinker thought, the sort of face that was easy to forget.

They came so close, they almost stepped on him. Instead, they veered downhill toward the water, heading for the shelter of two dense fir trees. Tinker could hear their voices although he could not see them through the screen of low branches. Now he remembered! They must be the two soldiers he and Clever-Lazy had overheard while they were lying in the cave.

"Eat good and stay dry, that's the secret of survival," he

heard the older man growl. "I'll wager we'll lose more men from fever while we're looking for the witch than if we had been sent with the others for a good honest fight. But not this old soldier. I ain't going to die in a miserable swamp."

"Lurky kind of place," said Bumpkin. "What would a sorceress be doing here?"

"Like draws to like. Some say there used to be a city here, palaces and temples all ruled by a witch queen who rode on a dragon. Certain times, folks say, you can look down in the water and see lights and people moving about."

"Do you believe that, Scar?"

"Who, me? Naw, that's just talk. But not the kind of talk I enjoy."

"Why do they make us keep looking for her? No woman's that important, eh? Eh, Scar?"

"I've been thinking about that. I don't think it's only the witch or only the dragon, though that's what *they* say. Minute I saw them fireworks, I got a prickle all along my scar. And when my scar pricks, I pay attention."

"That's because it's telling you something, ain't that right? Ain't that right, Scar?"

"It's telling me not to look at the obvious. So if I don't look at the sparks and flowers and pretty dragons in the sky, I start to look at what pushed them up there. If that push, that power, could be used to throw things from a distance, break down walls maybe, the Southies wouldn't know what hit them, eh? War would never be the same again. Change the rules. Change the world!"

"D'you mean the woman knows how to do that? Is that why they want us to take her alive? What if she won't tell?"

"She'll tell all right! They have their ways. They were all set to torture the old man who helped her escape. The old fool's heart cracked before they fair got started. But he probably didn't know anything about the fireworks. It's her we gotta catch. Just our luck to be sent to a place like this."

Tinker pressed himself against the damp earth. The perfume of earth and ferns and cedar was almost over-whelming. Even more overwhelming was his grief for Tax Collector, and gladness that their loyal old friend had not had to suffer long. He must get back to Clever-Lazy and tell her the news. He must get back to his wife for a thou-sand other reasons! Meanwhile, he was pinned to this exposed place on the hillside with two soldiers (and who knew how many more) between him and the river.

"I'm hungry, Scar. Let me go up to the camp and see if they're handing out rations."

"All you'll get is moldy rice," Scar warned. "But see what you can forage. I heard a fish jump and there are plenty of lilies; that means water chestnuts. If you can find some wild onions on the way back, we won't do so bad. Stick with me, boy, and eat good. Better than officer's mess, that's for sure."

Using Bumpkin's noisy climb up the hillside for cover, Tinker took the chance of stealing closer to the river. He watched in admiration as Scar set about his fishing. The man was wonderfully alert. He gazed into the depths with the piercing intensity of a kingfisher, then pounced and scooped so deftly that within minutes two plump trout lay on the bank. He cleaned them expertly with his dagger and then, with curious daintiness, laid them out in all their stippled splendor on a large green lily pad, and surrounded them with chestnutlike lily bulbs. During the entire maneuver, Scar never ceased to keep watch. He paused often to listen to the slightest sound, and even when there wasn't any sound. He stared across the river and into the underbrush, rubbing his cheek fiercely as he did so. By the time Bumpkin came back, his mood had changed for the worse.

"What did y'-hear up at the camp?"

"Same old rumors. We're stayin' here. We're movin' out. It's stopped raining, and some say if the waters go down, they'll make us form long lines and beat our way through the bush, same as hunting for wild boar."

When Scar gave forth a low growl, Tinker thought for a startled moment that he was hearing his own despairing moan. He must get away as soon as possible! He must find Clever-Lazy. He would run through the marsh calling her name. Under cover of darkness he might be able to find her before the trackers beat their way to her whereabouts. He wormed his way down the embankment.

"Hoy, what's that?" Scar paused in his eating, a piece of raw fish halfway to his mouth. He got up from where he was sitting and went down to the water's edge. He thought he saw a head bobbing in the current; the gloomy twilight hindered his vision. An otter? He rubbed his cheek thought-fully and went back to his meal. Several times during the night, he rose and returned to the river. The waters were receding after the flash flood. They gurgled, sucked, snick-ered in the moonless night. He thought he heard an owl cry. No, not an owl; some other, unknown, night bird. "Clever-Lazy, Clever-Lazy," it seemed to say.

Clever-Lazy thought she heard Tinker calling to her. She lay awake but with eyes closed trying to remember where she was. Her bed rocked gently beneath her and sud-denly she recalled going to sleep in the hollow log. She opened her eyes, expecting to see the crudely woven roof sticks and vines just above her nose; instead she found herself staring at a white dome far above her head. She tried to rise, but found she was bound by straps of some stretchy substance that enabled her to move fairly comfort-ably, but did not permit her to leave where she was lying. She knew she was no longer in her log, but whatever she was confined to was just as narrow. She closed her eyes, trying to figure out what had happened. There! Surely that was Tinker's voice, a long way off.

When next she opened her eyes the room was brighter, almost sunlit, but with a glare subtly different from sun-light. Awkwardly she struggled to her side and half raised herself on one elbow. She was lying on a high bench or table in a room that was otherwise bare of furniture. She studied the walls and ceiling carefully. She was in a cube-shaped chamber with a vaulted roof, but the ribs of the vault were cut short. Perhaps, she guessed, she was in the inmost section of a partitioned sphere.

A clicking noise called her attention to the wall behind her. Rubies, emeralds, topazes flashed and flickered there. Arranged in rows, each gem shone forth brilliantly one moment, lost all color the next. Clever-Lazy knew quite a lot about jewels. After all, she had lived at court and she had used gems in her experiments. But she had never seen jewels that flared and dulled themselves like these; jewels that danced and flickered to the music of clicks. Clever-Lazy had never seen an instrument panel.

"Tinker?" Her voice sounded creaky in her own ears. No one answered, but she gasped as an enormous ruby, almost as big as her head, slowly descended from the center of the ceiling. A cascade of soft rosy light shivered down the walls, caressed her body, filled the room. Still she felt a rise and fall, a gentle rocking that caused her to remember the log, the rain, a sense of being adrift. She forced herself not to close her eyes.

"Where am I?" she asked aloud. The only answer was the click-clicking of the jewels on the wall behind her. She blinked, shook her head. A section of the wall in front of her softened, became cloudy, melted into colors that swirled, parted, came together again in dreamlike floating patterns. Clever-Lazy caught a glimpse of her own face peering out as from a mirror, then it disappeared again, lost in a firestorm of color.

"Where am I?" she repeated. Rapid clicks: the mirror cleared and clouded several times and became a window. A fish swam by. Clever-Lazy wondered if she were staring into a goldfish bowl, but the fish was a pike, enormous. It disappeared among reed stalks thick as her wrist, white from lack of sun. White lily roots dangled from above and more fish swam by. Obviously, thought Clever-Lazy, she was beneath the surface of a pool or lake, perhaps a river.

Clever-Lazy closed her eyes, sank back. What had happened? She longed for a hug from Tinker. She sat up, spoke aloud. "Where is Tinker?" she asked. No answer. Suddenly she was angry. "Tell me where Tinker is right now!" she demanded. The window-mirror clouded, trembled, striped itself with fractured color. "Click-click-click" chattered the jewels on the far wall. The window-mirror cleared.

Clever-Lazy saw a man crouched low, running. Tinker! She could hear him panting, almost sobbing as he fled through the swamp. Her view widened. Tinker became smaller, more distant. 'I must be a bird,' she thought. 'I am here in this strange room; at the same time, I am a bird watching the marsh from a great height.' She could still see Tinker as he ran through the reeds. Behind him, a long line of soldiers advanced shoulder-to-shoulder, or at least they tried to. They had great difficulty maintaining their marching order as they stomped through the mud, hopped over trickles, parted before trees and brambles. They had to swerve to avoid the deepest pools.

Clever-Lazy watched in horror as one man actually

stepped into a pool. She saw him go down; she saw the others part, then close their ranks as though he had never been. She saw him rise to the surface twice, then sink again, helpless in his heavy armor. Behind the men she saw the officers on horseback, shouting orders, cracking whips. Behind the officers lumbered a large and patient elephant.

Behind the elephant, at some distance, she saw two more men. One was tall, young, bony, the other older and thick-set. When the older man turned his head, which he did frequently, she swooped down for a closer look. A livid scar snaked down the side of his nose and across one cheek. In his right hand he held an onion from which he took frequent hearty bites; from his left hand dangled a rabbit, head down. The two companions positively sauntered. They kept just far enough behind the elephant to be out of sight in the reeds, yet close enough to the main procession so they would not be lost.

As she watched, the older man stopped suddenly, turned and looked straight at her. For a moment, she thought he *must* see her, so sharply did he peer into the space in front of him. A puzzled expression spread over his battered countenance. He sighed, shrugged his shoulders and reached up an oniony hand to rub his itching scar. Then the whole scene flickered, wavered and faded from the wall.

Night had come again. Tinker had doubled back behind the line of men and returned to the part of the marsh where he was still convinced he would find his wife. He hardly cared whether or not he was discovered. All he wanted was to find Clever-Lazy. He almost wished the soldiers would find her for him just to relieve his worst fears; then he realized how crazy such a hope was. He was wet and hungry and so weary that he couldn't think straight. He floundered ahead, staggering through the moonless night, calling and calling. Snags reached out to trip him; briers tore at his hair and clothes; reeds, sharp as swords, drew blood from his bare skin. Desperate and unheeding, he came ever closer to the largest, deepest and most treacherous pool in the marsh.

Scar and Bumpkin were lost in the marsh, too. Scar had outsmarted himself. He had paused to build a fire to roast his rabbit, and had let the company get so far ahead that he and Bumpkin were caught by the darkness. They had found a dry spot where two or three trees grew together, and there they had had their feast. The trees were near a deep pool too big to go around in the dark. Bumpkin did not like the place. He wanted to keep the fire going to add a little cheer, but Scar decided against it. He did not know why, exactly, but he scratched his cheek (which had itched unbearably the last few days) and became his most stubborn self.

This was the second night Scar could not sleep. Bumpkin snored away, but Scar sat bolt upright in the darkness, his back against a tree, his ears cocked for every sound. There it was again! That cursed night bird had a wail that sounded almost human. "Clever-Lazy, Clever-Lazy." Very close it was. Something big was splashing through the swamp.

Again Clever-Lazy heard her husband calling her name. She sat up and cried out, "Tinker, I'm here!" The jewels on the wall clicked into action at the sound of her voice. "Show me my husband," she commanded. A moment later, the wall in front of her melted, clouded and showed Tinker running straight toward her. His face was white and anguished even in the darkness, and she knew he was about to fall into the deep pool where she was lying. He would drown unless she saved him! She cried out in terror and struggled against the straps that bound her.

"Tinker, watch out! Tinker, go back!" The jewels on the wall flashed furiously. She did not beg. She commanded. "Save him! Save him!"

Scar sprang up in alarm, his dagger already drawn. With his free hand, he reached down and shook Bumpkin awake. The younger man stared wide-eyed into the darkness.

"What is it? What's going on?"

"Shut up, you idiot! Listen!"

A man blundered into the clearing. He came straight at them. They could see his white face and great fearful eyes; then he was gone so quickly that Scar lowered his dagger in self-disgust. The next moment they heard a splash. The man must have fallen into the pool. They could hear him struggling. They crept forward and peered through the brambles. A light, a dim low light, shone out. Scar could not guess where it came from, but it made the water glitter like carved jet. Now they could see a huge twisted snag that leaned out over the pool. The man who had run past them was caught in its writhing roots.

Scar pointed to the center of the pool. Bumpkin whimpered. The light in the pool grew and grew. Something huge and shining was emerging, did emerge, from the depths, floated on the surface. A terrible face shone upon the waters, and two enormous eyes sent out beams of light that swept the banks. Scar and Bumpkin stumbled back, shielding their faces with uplifted arms. The awful gaze lingered, lighting up the trees and brush as bright as day, then swerved away from them to focus on the man struggling with the snag.

"Is it a dragon, Scar?"

Scar did not answer. He was watching as two long arms, hinged at the elbow, reached out their claws toward the man. With awe-inspiring strength and cunning, one claw pulled the rotten trunk from the bank while the other's bony fingers delicately plucked man from snag. Like meat from a bone, Scar told himself.

The man struggled frantically, but it was no use. The creature opened its giant maw, revealing a mouthful of jewels and fire. The next moment, the mouth had closed, the man had disappeared. The creature rose from the water noiselessly, effortlessly. Straight up it rose in the night sky, and for the first time in many nights the full moon shone down on earth.

Bumpkin let out a great sigh of relief and turned to look at the moon. "Whew! I spooked myself. I haven't seen the moon for so long, and in this creepy place even the reflection scared me. I thought I saw . . ." He gave a high-pitched laugh. "Scar, you wouldn't believe what I thought I saw."

But Scar was not looking at the moon. He had turned his eyes from that familiar spectacle and was watching a second shining object, unidentifiable, streak across the sky.

20

The Dancing Mountains

CLEVER-LAZY AND TINKER awoke on a cold hill-side. Mist swirled about them, confusion swirled in their heads. Clever-Lazy felt that she had been in a long sleep. Tinker could not remember anything after he had been plucked from the snag. They did not speak of what had happened in the marsh.

Sun burned through the mist. The outline of familiar peaks made them know they were in the foothills of the Dancing Mountains. Somewhere below them was Clever-Lazy's native village. As they climbed upward, Clever-Lazy was able to point out landmarks that had been pointed out to her the day she and her parents visited the shrine of the Goddess. Now, however, she was no longer a girl going to celebrate her fifteenth birthday; she was a woman, a woman soon to have a child. She was glad to accept Tinker's help from time to time, but fortunately she was strong and healthy, much used to travel. She did not ask for help often.

Two nights and a day had passed by the time they reached the top of their mountain. They lay together under the pine tree, enjoying the light of the waning moon, and talked about what they would do now that they had reached their destination. About the mysterious events which had brought them here, they said nothing.

"As soon as it is light," promised Clever-Lazy, "I shall show you the shrine of the Goddess."

"As soon as we have seen the Goddess," promised Tinker, "we shall look for a place to live. Winter is coming and we need shelter for the baby." They fell asleep listening to the wind in the pine tree, the sound of a hidden waterfall.

In the morning, they drank from the stream that trickled to the cliff edge and Tinker set a snare to catch a rabbit. He had felt about in his pack for a few grains of rice by way of breakfast, knowing even as he did so that there was no food left. Clever-Lazy, who was always hungry these days, for once did not complain. Instead, she was so eager to enter the shrine that she stood by the stone that looked like a half-opened door and urged him to hurry. Tinker hung back.

"What does the Goddess look like?" he inquired, suddenly fearful.

"I've never seen her," replied Clever-Lazy.

"But the image, the idol, how does it look? Is it . . . she . . . big or little? Young or old? Beautiful or hideous?"

"I don't know," said Clever-Lazy. "I stood behind my mother and looked over her shoulder. All I saw was shadow. But today, in this bright sunlight, we'll really be able to see her. Oh, Tinker, I've waited all my life for this moment!"

Clever-Lazy took Tinker's hand and led him around the stone to the cool shadowed space on the other side. Directly in front of them was the mouth of a shallow cave. Clever-Lazy knelt heavily, her movements made awkward by the child. Tinker fell to his knees a little way behind her. He watched his wife warily, seeking clues as to what he should do next. He no longer scoffed, and he was determined to do what was meet and right. Above all else, he longed for the Goddess to approve of him.

Clever-Lazy reminded the Goddess of her parents' death and thanked her for answering the prayer she had made on her fifteenth birthday. "O Goddess, with your help I am no longer a mere dumpling. With your help I have grown up and married Tinker and become an inventor." Then she thanked the Goddess for the chance to have a workshop. When she thought of the workshop, she became aware of a dull ache of resentment. Never again would she have the time and space and equipment to pursue her ideas, the encouragement to conduct her experiments. "Now I'm going to have a baby," she told the Goddess. Then she paused, wondering what to say next. Nothing occurred to her so she nudged Tinker.

Tinker cleared his throat. "O Goddess," he prayed, "thank you for sending us a child. Teach me to be a good husband and father, and let us live on your mountain in good health and happiness so we never have to travel the roads again. And if you know how we can get through the winter, please let me know."

Tinker had asked for what he wanted. Clever-Lazy had wanted to ask for her workshop. But she didn't. It would have seemed ungrateful. The Goddess had saved them from torture and death, and she was going to have a baby. Why couldn't she feel as glad as Tinker did?

Tinker raised his head, wondering what revelation there would be. He helped Clever-Lazy struggle to her feet and they stood leaning against each other. Then, holding hands, peering into the shadows, they went forward into the cave.

There was nothing there.

Clever-Lazy could not, would not believe the cave was empty. Well, not quite empty. There was a stone pillar, hardly more than a crudely chiseled rock, that rose naturally from the stone floor. The top of it was flat and might have, at one time, held some sort of figure or idol. Now there was nothing. She emerged into the sunlight blinking away tears. Her mother had lied to her!

Tinker, who did not know whether to be bitter or consoling, kept quiet. Against his better judgment, he told himself, he had allowed himself to be led astray by his wife's crazy beliefs and superstitions. He had not expected miracles, but he had hoped that there would be a cave or, perhaps, a ruined temple where they could find a haven for the winter. He busied himself with the rabbit he had caught, skinning it and setting it to roast, while he considered what their next move should be.

Clever-Lazy did not speak during the meal. She ate hungrily but mechanically. After they had eaten, they set about to explore. At one time, the mountain must have risen to a rounded peak but part of that had been cleared away, leaving the little plateau where they now stood. The cave where they had expected to find the Goddess entered into the peak's rocky remnant or tor. In front of the tor, hiding the cave, stood the tall, doorlike stone. At the other end of the plateau was a clump of low firs, rhododendron, and bamboo. A spring rose among the thick-growing bushes. The little stream that issued from it ran only a few yards before plunging over the edge of the cliff.

Together they stood and watched the fall of water. Trees and outcroppings hid the place where the water struck, but by listening carefully, they thought they could judge its distance far below. Tinker squinted at the morning sun. By afternoon it would work its way around to shine on the other face of the mountain. The ledge below would be warmed both by the sun and the reflection from the cliff. Perhaps they could find a place to survive the winter after all. "Clever-Lazy," he said, "I'm going to climb down the cliff and explore the next level. Then I'll come back for you."

Clever-Lazy, remembering the experience in the swamp, refused to be separated. She argued that she had climbed down a cliff before, from the Dragon's Hole to the great plain beneath. Despite Tinker's arguments Clever-Lazy was stubborn. "If I don't have the Goddess anymore, Tinker, you are everything I have. I would rather be killed going down the cliff than left here on the mountaintop, wondering what has happened to you." She shivered, remembering the experience in the marsh.

The descent took hours. Clever-Lazy was less agile than she had been a few months before. When they reached the bottom and followed the stream forward, they came to another steep drop. They were on a ledge that, although it was wide enough to support a good growth of trees, was a much narrower space than Tinker had hoped for. There would be no room to farm, and the few rabbits isolated on the ledge would soon be hunted out. They would be marooned here as if it were a small island.

Tinker looked up at the hard smoothness of the cliff above them and wondered how they had ever managed to get down. His wife was exhausted. She complained that now she was ready to call a halt, her baby was kicking from inside. They could not go back but neither could they go forward, at least not before a night's rest. They curled up in a pile of leaves and fell into restless sleep.

Clever-Lazy awoke in the morning with a feeling of heavy sadness. She was surprised to find tears upon her cheeks, and could not imagine what they were for until she remembered the empty cave. Not even when her parents died had she experienced such grief. Now not only the Goddess, but her father and mother, seemed infinitely far away, almost as though they had never existed. She lay with her eyes closed, trying to summon strength and courage to open them and start the day.

When at last she struggled to sit up, she found that Tinker was already awake. He had found some nuts and berries, which he was arranging on a flat laurel leaf for her breakfast. He told her how he had watched Scar fussing daintily as he placed trout and water chestnuts on a lily pad. For the first time each began to talk, albeit cautiously, about what had happened in the marsh. Clever-Lazy tried to explain how she had seen a soldier with a scarred face, perhaps the same man, staring straight at her, almost nose-to-nose. The man could not see her although she could see him, and yet she was sure he had been vaguely aware of her presence. When Tinker refused to believe her, she relapsed into silence.

The sun would not warm the ledge until later in the day. They were glad to get moving. They followed the stream to its new jumping-off place, and saw below them a deep pool surrounded by trees and high rock; what lay beyond was hard to tell. Again they edged their way down a precipice. Toward the bottom, among fallen rocks, they found stones that looked as though they had been worked by tools, perhaps part of a staircase that had for some reason been hastily demolished.

Stepping from rock to rock, they picked their way around the pool to the far end. The stream fell steeply through a wooded glen and came out into a valley. As it widened, Tinker pointed out the hint of once-terraced fields. They could see the glint of other waterfalls, and Clever-Lazy's eye was caught by plumes of smoke or mist that rose straight up from the valley floor. When they approached one of these, they discovered not human habitation, but a hot spring bubbling up from beneath the earth. As they advanced, flocks of birds rose up almost at their feet, a herd of antelope turned to stare, wild pigs scuttled into the underbrush. Sometime in the afternoon Tinker touched his wife on the shoulder and pointed to a ruined wall shining in the sun.

In the weeks before the first snow, Tinker worked frantically to restore a corner of the ruined building. He was determined that they should have shelter for the winter and a place for the baby to be born. Clever-Lazy helped as much as she could, but the heaviness of her spirit, as much as her body, seemed to get in the way.

The only thing that interested her was the mosaic floor that she discovered when she was digging away an accumulation of leaves and dirt and broken tiles. A hot spring surged nearby, and enough of the inventor in her was stirred to work out a way in which steam and hot water could be run under the mosaic floor to heat their quarters during the winter. When Tinker began to dig, he found a system of gutters already installed. To make the heat flow, they had only to clean out the debris of centuries and replace parts of the channels with broken roof tiles and flat pebbles from the stream.

Clever-Lazy was fascinated by the mosaic, and spent hours lying on the warm floor studying the complicated picture made up of thousands of pieces of colored stone. The background was deep blue, the color of sky. Undulating lines plunging down both sides suggested a river. At the bottom was the ocean, above it a border of green hills and prism-shaped mountain peaks. Vermilion temples and gold pagodas sprang from these to be half hidden in a wilderness of stylized flowers, trees and exotic birds.

Floating in the blue mosaic sky, was a huge dragon face with large staring eyes and an open mouth. A cloud of fire surrounded the head and two claws extended. Tinker turned away with a shudder. He could not bear to look at it.

"That's what I saw the night we were leaving the Dragon's Hole," said Clever-Lazy. "Do you think that's what brought us to the Dancing Mountains?" Tinker did not like to think, much less talk, about such an awful possibility.

But little by little they did talk. Each told the other what had happened in the marsh, and tried to piece together their separate adventures. Clever-Lazy described the inside of the sphere, the glare of its whiteness, the suspended ruby, the clicking jewels. She tried to describe the window-mirror through or on which she had watched Tinker as he ran for his life. Tinker could only shake his head. Everything she had seen had actually happened to him. But Clever-Lazy had no memory of his being plucked from the snag, eaten by the dragon. "What did it look like?" she asked. For answer her husband pointed to the head that floated in the blue sky of the mosaic.

At the very end of winter, the baby was born. The birthing was neither hard nor easy; there was pain but not too much to bear. 'Good honest work,' thought Clever-Lazy as she pushed the child forth. Tinker was there to comfort her and to catch the baby. He tied the cord into a neat belly button and cut it with the same deftness and sense of timing he showed in everything else he did. Only afterwards did he begin to tremble and feel weak in the knees at the knowledge that they had a son.

Clever-Lazy had expected more joy. She remembered or tried to remember everything her mother had told her about her own birth. According to her parents, she had been round and plump, dimpled and sweet-tempered, a source of happiness. The child that Tinker placed in her arms was red and scrawny. Sometimes he arched his back and screamed; he would not even stop when she put him to her breast. She called him Noisemaker.

Clever-Lazy knew no more about looking after a baby than she had known about housework. Every day Tinker either went to the fields to scratch out a garden patch or he went hunting. Every day and every night Clever-Lazy looked after Noisemaker. She grew tired and depressed. She listened dully to Tinker's plans for the future. They quarreled often, and Clever-Lazy wept.

Tinker was worried because he had so little to plant; they needed a seed crop. He proposed that he climb the mountainside the way they had come down, and that he make his way into towns and villages that lay beyond the village where Clever-Lazy had grown up. Her village had marked the farthest extent of his route, and he hoped that in new territory no one would know him. Certainly his appearance had changed. He was more muscular and weathered; he had grown a beard and his hair was long and loose. He dressed in skins and furs. He did not have to disguise himself to look like a mountain man. He was one.

Tinker talked excitedly of his plans. He had hunted all winter; now he planned to trade the pelts for rice seedlings, millet, beans. He would take with him chunks of malachite and other ores, semi-precious stones and jade that he had mined himself. He hoped to bring back articles they did not know how to make — woven cloth, pots and baskets. He would also try to bring back a few coins for future use. If he were successful, he told his wife, they and their children's children would be able to live for years in their hidden valley.

"I have never been so happy," said Tinker. "If there were a Goddess, I would thank her for giving me everything I asked for."

'I have never felt so miserable,' thought Clever-Lazy, 'and I don't know what I want.'

21

The Dark Tower

EXCEPT AT NIGHT when she slept alone, Clever-Lazy hardly noticed that Tinker was gone. She arose at the usual time, did her usual chores, fixed meals for herself and looked after Noisemaker. After all, she spent most of her days alone anyway. But on the third day, when the sun shone, birds sang and fat buds burst into green and gold, Clever-Lazy caught spring fever. Above all else, she longed to be with Tinker, not so much for love of him as for what he was doing. How unfair, she thought, that he should be the one to leave the valley, especially since he did not really want to go. It was she who yearned to travel new roads, see new sights, mingle with people.

Tinker had already explored the far side of their valley. He reported to her that beyond the cliffs was a narrow ridge, another drop and desolate mountains. The easiest way to get back to the world of people and trading was to climb the cliff they had come down. To help him, Clever-Lazy invented pitons, and Tinker forged the two iron spikes that he could drive into the rock to give himself foothold. As soon as he had footing on the higher one, he could haul up the one below by means of a leather thong and hammer it into the rock facing a step above. Thus, foot by foot, he made his way up the cliff.

Clever-Lazy invented those pitons, but she had not let herself ask Tinker to make a pair for her, nor did he offer to do so. One way she stopped herself from asking was to decide beforehand that Tinker would refuse. There was no way out; she must stay behind and look after their baby. She sighed and a tear stole down her cheek. What was wrong with her? Secretly she had convinced herself that she was a bad mother. Even Shopshrewd had had more motherly feeling!

On the fourth day, she began to talk to Noisemaker. "Do you know," she said, "I think it may be my birthday. I feel it in my bones that either today or tomorrow is the right day to celebrate. When my parents were alive . . ." She paused, corrected herself. "When your grandparents were alive, they used to make a great fuss of my birthday. The best birthday and the last I ever spent with them, they brought me to the Dancing Mountains. To see the Goddess . . ." Again she paused, this time to blink away tears.

After she had fed and tidied her baby, Clever-Lazy put him down on a rug on the warm floor to amuse himself. Noisemaker seemed to watch her as she did her chores. Now that he was almost three months old she had more idea of what to expect from him. He no longer woke in the middle of the night, and she had more sense of when he would sleep and eat and be awake. Perhaps he was more used to her, too. When he drifted into his morning nap, she took some skins from the pile that Tinker had brought her, and managed to cobble up a not-too-unsatisfactory shoulder bag. Into it she put enough food to last her several days. When Noisemaker woke up, she nursed him again, bathed him and wrapped him in a pouch of rabbit skins. "Today," she said, "I am going to teach you to be clever. Today we are going to be lazy." Then she put the new bag over her shoulder, hoisted Noisemaker to her back and set off on a journey of her own.

"There must be some way for me to get out of the valley," Clever-Lazy told herself. She followed the stream and climbed through the woods toward the noise of the waterfall. Instead of staying in the dark glen that led to the pool, she scrambled up the bank and followed the forest level to the base of the cliff. The granite rising above her looked as smooth as glass. She walked along the cliff, inspecting it closely. Here and there rock seams or cracks afforded perilous hold, but she had to admit that ascent would be impossible with a baby on her back. Not even pitons would be much help, and she would be putting the baby in terrible danger.

She needed time to think. Clever-Lazy sat down on a sun-warmed boulder. No longer lulled by the motion of her walk, Noisemaker awoke and protested shrilly. He wouldn't allow her even a few minutes to herself! Sighing, she lowered him from her back and spread his fur wrappings on the stone. With almost grudging admiration, she watched as he lay on his back and kicked in the sunshine. His arms and legs had filled out. He was getting positively plump. She wished her mother could see him, or Bowlmaker or even Shopshrewd. She wished she still believed in the Goddess; the Goddess would see what a beautiful child he was. She leaned down to touch her baby's soft cheek. It was then she saw the disk and spiral carved into the stone.

Clever-Lazy caught her breath, then raised her head to look around her. From long habit she looked for a sighting, an alignment with something else that had to do with the dragon. In one direction lay the pool and the fallen steps. If she stood in line with the steps and looked over the boulder, her eye continued to where the cliff ledge stopped, dropping off sheer beneath the peak. She bundled Noisemaker into his skins, slung him on her back and started off again.

When she came to the place where the land narrowed, she had to edge her way along, clinging to the cliff. At last, she came to what she was looking for, another carving in the rock. Now there was no other place to go; granite rose above her to the peak, beneath was nothing but cloud. It was almost like being alongside the prow of a great ship. She looked around her worriedly. Mist was everywhere, obscuring the way she had come. Now that the sun kept itself hidden, the air was bitingly cold. Moreover the mist was changing to sleety rain.

Clever-Lazy was anxious and concerned for her baby. She was not at all sure exactly how fragile babies are. She knew for certain she did not want him to spend the night on a cold mountain ledge. Noisemaker lifted his voice and bawled. She tried feeding him; she tried rocking him; she tried singing to him. Nothing she did seemed to help. 'Why couldn't she be like other mothers? Why didn't she know by instinct what to do?'

She was sitting with her back to the weather, facing the cliff so as to shelter her baby as much as possible. Her nose was almost against the carving. Whether she wanted to or not, she could hardly avoid studying the design minutely. A face peered out from its center, the same face set into the mosaic on the steam-warmed floor of their pavilion. She reached out a hand wonderingly. 'Oh, to be warm again!' she thought. At the same moment Noisemaker gave a piercing, high-pitched scream, and Clever-Lazy felt the rock move, then pivot inward at her touch.

Holding her child in her arms, Clever-Lazy stepped over the stone sill. The door shut behind her with a click. She turned and tried to open it again, but it would not give. "If we can't go back, we might as well go forward," she said aloud. Her voice echoed hollowly. She slung Noisemaker on her back and felt her way step-by-step. As her eyes grew more accustomed to the dim light, she saw that she was in a long gallery or corridor. Rock spar and sheep silver shone faintly on the walls. The air was neither cold nor warm; assuredly it was better than rain and mist. She stepped out more boldly.

Almost imperceptibly the corridor wound upward. Sometimes there were steps; overhead, rough vaults and arches. Obviously this was not a natural formation, but had been designed and made by human hands. Far away she could hear the drip and trickle of water over rock. She could not make out where the twilight came from, but the air was fresh and there continued to be enough light for her to see her surroundings.

She had no idea how long she had been climbing when she came to a flight of steps that rose in a steep spiral. Each wedge-shaped step was so narrow that she had to place her feet sideways to make the ascent, leaning inward to balance the weight of the baby. Several times when she felt herself wobbling, she braced herself in a half-sitting position on the wider part of a step in order to regain breath as well as balance.

Above her she could see a round hole. 'It's as though I were climbing up a well,' thought Clever-Lazy. As she neared the top, first her shoulders, then her head emerged into a large vaulted space. Arches soared upward from slender pillars. 'We must be under the tor, the very top of the mountain,' she guessed. Still standing on the steps, she unslung Noisemaker from her back and set him carefully on the stone floor. He stirred slightly, half-awakened by the unaccustomed lack of motion. Once certain he was safe and would not roll, she placed her hands, palms down, on the smooth surface and swung herself up to his level.

When she looked about her, she saw that the room was lofty but not enormous. The rounded dome, the sense of carefully proportioned enclosure, reminded her of some other place; she was not sure what or where. Noisemaker whimpered. She picked him up and carried him to the center of the room. Three upright stones stood in a rough circle or triangle there, each higher than her head. Suspended over them was a slender stalactite, an icicle-shaped spear of crystallized minerals. She sat down and leaned her back against one of the standing stones, and gave the baby her breast. She was hungry and thirsty herself. She must take time to eat! Noisemaker could only eat if she did.

She cocked her ear to the sound of trickling water. After she had nursed her child, she put him to sleep in the stone circle and went in search while he slept. A channel had been carved across the rock floor. Clear water had collected in a stone-rimmed pool, hardly more than a basin. She drank deeply. On the way back to the center of the room, she kicked something that skittered along the floor. The room was darker now; perhaps night had come. She had difficulty finding what she had kicked and, when she picked it up, she had trouble seeing what it was. A bone! Shuddering, she threw it aside and returned to the center of the room, picked up her baby and hugged him to her. After awhile, when nothing happened, she put the baby down and took out a packet of food. When she had eaten, she spread out her cloak, took Noisemaker into the crook of her arm, and slept.

When she awoke she thought for a moment that she was back in the hollow sphere, a prisoner under water, then knew that she was somewhere else oddly like it. Something red and rosy gleamed above her, almost, but not quite, as the great light had shone in the underwater sphere. A shaft of icy white calcite embedded with rubies as big as plums hung from the ceiling above her head. Half-awake, still not quite convinced she was not in the sphere, her eyes sought out the panel of clicking lights. Ah, there!

She left Noisemaker asleep in his rabbit skins and went over to the wall. Minerals and dampness had hardened to a thin crust, but something bright and bumpy gleamed underneath. She chipped away at the thin shell. One by one the jewels shone out, ruby and topaz and emerald embedded in a regular pattern in the rock. These real jewels reacted to reflected light, not the transparent kind that had danced and clicked when she was prisoner in the sphere.

She looked around in awe and wonder. Perhaps someone had made the sphere in imitation of this strange domed chamber, perhaps the room had been made in imitation of the sphere. She turned around to face the center of the room again, toward the circle of stones beneath the stalactite. Noisemaker still slept, oblivious. Either the light was less dim than it had been the previous day, or her eyes were more accustomed to their surroundings. One of the stones looked to her like a woman's head and bust. She could see the profile quite distinctly. As she neared the stones again she could see the images of three women, their heads and shoulders. They faced inward to the center of the circle, bending slightly as though to look down on the sleeping child.

One of the images was of an old woman; one a woman about the age of her mother as she remembered her; the third represented a young woman, hardly more than a girl. Clever-Lazy slipped between two of the statues into the center again. If the panel of jewels was behind her, then the mirror-window should be in front, on the opposite wall. She crossed the room and peered at the rocky surface. She closed her eyes, felt with her fingertips, found a large area of unnatural flatness. She rubbed her ragged sleeve against it, saw a bit of shine. Surely this was a mirror, a bronze mirror! It was like, yet unlike, the mirror-window she had seen before. She decided to test it.

"Show me my husband. Show me Tinker," commanded Clever-Lazy. Nothing happened. There were no clicks from the panel of jewels, no window to the outside world, no amazing pictures of scenes far away. The light in the room had become brighter now. The tall stones behind her were reflected in the polished bronze.

Could she have been mistaken? The stones in the center of the room were not huge busts but full length figures, only slightly larger than life-size. Looking carefully at the one closest to her, she perceived that what had seemed to be sculpted locks of hair were now something else — an uplifted arm, a fold of clothing, an out-thrust leg. Yet, by shifting her own body ever so little, she could still see the profile of the woman who looked like her mother.

But now she saw other figures, images, portraits. There was an infinity of women! She moved back and forth between the mirror and the circle, experimenting. As she moved she caught glimpses of women she knew, women she had seen only once or casually, women she was sure she had never seen. She blinked her eyes, willing herself to shift her vision. What was figure became ground, then a new figure emerged from the background and the old figure slipped away. Even the spaces between the stones took on shape, became negatives outlined in stone, then melted into space again. Not only did it make a difference where she stood and from what angle she perceived, but her own body became part of the composition.

Just a few hours before, she had wished that her mother and Bowlmaker could see her baby. Now it seemed as though they were here, bending forward to admire him. She saw Shopshrewd and Little Prune, Ever Curious and Not Quite, Ascending One's wife and ladies of the court. She saw a shadowy figure she was almost positive must be Tax Collector's wife. She saw a scrawny woman stevedore, naked to the waist. She saw the Emperor's concubines and the fluttering girls from the House of Flowers. She saw a woman who had given her something to eat that first night she told stories on the streets. She saw women she had passed in crowds, girlish faces, faces from her childhood. She saw the Proud Maiden. She saw herself.

'If there is a Goddess,' thought Clever-Lazy, 'then every woman is part of her and she is part of every woman.'

Next moment, she was hurrying across the floor to Noisemaker. He was awake, he was hungry and he was letting her know.

22

A Joyful Noise

AFTER SHE HAD fed him, Clever-Lazy took Noisemaker in her arms and circled the room. She was looking for a way out. She found the bone she had flung aside the night before. In daylight, it was not as sinister as she had imagined. It was hollow and perforated with drilled holes. By placing her fingers over the holes and blowing at one end, she was able to make of it a musical pipe or whistle.

Noisemaker was delighted. So delighted that he gurgled and made little soft laughing sounds that Clever-Lazy had never heard before. She spread out the rabbit skins for him and let him kick his heels while she experimented. When he made a noise, she tried to imitate it, at least its pitch, as best she could. When he made another sort of noise, she tried to follow again. Then *she* played a note and *he* seemed to respond.

Oh, the cleverness of him! She had never seen such a

beautiful and intelligent child! A feeling rushed over her that was akin to the feeling she had had when she put her arms around the small boy in Ascending One's courtyard, but this feeling was a thousand times more powerful. Joy and relief were mixed together. All along she had feared that she was a bad mother, but now she knew that she was not. She loved Noisemaker with all her heart and knew she always would.

She laughed and then he laughed. He let out a shriek, a squeal of pure joy. She copied it with a piercing whistle. She heard a scraping sound and smelled a sudden rush of damp, stale air. A stone had turned inward, pivoting on its axis to reveal a dark entrance. She rushed toward it, peered in and caught a glimpse of a short passageway terminated by steps. She hesitated. How damp and cramped and forbidding it looked! If she were to take advantage of this unexpected opening, she would have to wrap Noisemaker in his skins and go back to the center of the room to rescue her bag. The door closed with a click.

The moment she heard the click, she knew that above all else she wanted to go through that door. "Open!" she commanded. She pounded on the stony wall but all she got for her effort was a scraped fist. She tried feeling for the outlines of the door and was not certain she could distinguish it from other cracks in the rock. She went back for her bag and bundled up Noisemaker. Then she sat facing the wall as she nursed him and tried to think what to do next.

She remembered how she had sat facing the cliffside when she and Noisemaker were caught in the mist outside the mountain. Then there had been a dragon face carved in the rock. The door had opened when she touched the carving, but here there was no carving. She looked down at Noisemaker. He had finished nursing. Sated, he lay back with a drunken grin, tiny bubbles purling at the corner of his mouth. Now he seemed so content, but when they were on the mountainside, he had almost driven her out of her mind with his screams.

Screams? Noisemaker had been screaming when the door in the mountain opened; he had screamed again just as this door swung open. The first had been a scream of rage, the most recent a shriek of delight but the results had been the same. Perhaps there was a certain vibration that he set going that could cause the doors to open. She glanced down at her child. He was sound asleep. She shook him gently, trying to waken him, then giggled aloud with a mixture of guilt and amusement. For the first time since he had been born, she *wanted* Noisemaker to wake up and cry! She was about to try screaming herself when she remembered the whistling bone.

She had to try several times before she hit the right pitch, but when she did she found herself staring into the same musty passageway. She really did not like the idea of going in there. What if she were trapped and could not get out either end? She allowed the door to shut and open several times before gathering up the sleeping baby, the bag, the bone. She blew on the whistle. The door opened. She drew a deep breath and stepped over the sill.

The way was dark and suffocatingly narrow. She had to

rely on touch to make her way forward. Her main fear was that she and her child might get stuck or not be able to turn around. She came to the steps, then a landing. She could not imagine where she was. She could be in a coffin or a tomb. She fumbled for the whistle and blew a high ear-splitting note.

"O Goddess," she prayed, "make it work!"

When the door opened, Clever-Lazy found herself blinking in strong sunlight. As her eyes became accustomed to the sunshine, she stared into the mouth of a shallow cave. She was looking into the stony recess where she had once expected to find an image of the Goddess.

She was so astonished that she almost forgot to step forward. When she did so, she turned and looked at the gray-green stone that loomed like a huge door ajar in front of the cave. Why, it *was* a door! Or, rather, there was a door in it. She peered closely and saw a faint carving, an encircled spiral, traced into the rock. Always before, she had stood with her back to the standing stone, and had looked for the Goddess in the cave. She had never thought to look for a door in a stone shaped like a door.

A few days later Tinker, returning from his journey, pulled himself up to the top of the mountain and found his wife and child there. How dare Clever-Lazy risk her life and that of their child by climbing the steep cliff! When she assured him she had found a safer way to reach the mountaintop, he could make neither head nor tail of her hasty explanation.

"After you've rested and I fix something for you to eat," she said, "I'll show you what I've found. But before that, you must tell me of your own journey."

She persuaded him to lie under the pine tree and watch Noisemaker while she busied herself with gathering and preparing their food. Tinker lay on his back and found himself idly observing a wind chime she had fashioned out of short lengths of bamboo. The chime hung from a low branch and was attached to Noisemaker's wrist by a ribbon of soft, braided grass. From time to time, the baby waved his arms in the air and followed with bright knowing eyes the dangling toy. As soon as the chime fell silent, he jangled it again.

Tinker was charmed by the cleverness of his own child. Noisemaker had grown and changed even in the week his father had been away. Clever-Lazy had changed, too, Tinker noticed. She seemed so much more confident in the way she took care of the child. Her eyes were sparkling, her cheeks rosy, she chattered enthusiastically. "I'm teaching Noisemaker how to be lazy successfully," she said. When she giggled, he knew that he had his own dear Clever-Lazy back again.

Tinker told how he had struck out for new territory and had gone into villages where he had never been before. He had little fear of being recognized, but had been cautious nonetheless. People had accepted him as a mountain dweller, a hunter and trapper; he had been careful not to reveal any of his tinker's skills or special knowledge of worked metals. Not wishing to appear as a settled farmer, he had bartered for only a small amount of seed in any one village. The ore and jade had been dispensed with cannily, and he had brought back both coin and a few manufactured articles.

"I thought it would look suspicious if I never traded for metal objects. Most mountain men need knives so I accepted them in trade. We can always use a few extra. But it's cloth and baskets and pottery we need most. You never were much good at learning how to make ordinary things, Clever-Lazy."

His wife flushed. "I can learn," she said. "Since living here, I have come to appreciate how extraordinary these objects are. I wish I had watched Bowlmaker more carefully. To bring back the process is more important than hauling the objects up here. I'll go down the mountain soon and watch the weavers and potters and basket makers for myself. It seems so ridiculous that I can make a complicated clock for the Emperor, but I don't know how to weave a piece of cloth. I have more respect now for all those inventors who went before me."

Tinker was emphatic. "Clever-Lazy, I will not give you permission to leave the mountain. You must stay here and look after Noisemaker. You must learn to be a good mother."

"I *am* a good mother," returned Clever-Lazy. "And it's because I know I am that I will go out into the world from time to time. You can learn to look after Noisemaker just as well as I can."

"But I can't nurse him."

"Soon he'll be able to eat solid foods, and I don't think

it will be long before he can drink from a cup. I think we could get milk from wild sheep or antelope . . ."

Now Tinker was outraged. "Do you want our child to grow up to be an animal?" His feelings were far from soothed when Clever-Lazy only laughed at his fears.

"Oh, Tinker. At first all three of us can travel together if you like. But sooner or later I'll leave the mountain by myself. I will always come back, but I know I have to go. I *want* to go."

"It's not respectable for a woman to travel alone," retorted Tinker lamely.

"That's what you said when you found me living in the streets," she returned. "I'm glad you took me to Shopshrewd, but I'm not a little girl anymore. I want to go and visit Bowlmaker and learn how to make pots."

After she had told him of her adventure inside the tor, she led him to the gray-green standing stone and blew the whistle. Tinker was speechless. "I really believe," said Clever-Lazy, "that we will be able to open all the doors that lead back to our valley just by blowing the right pitch on this whistle."

"How did you learn to do that?" asked Tinker.

"Noisemaker showed me how."

It took some arguing, but finally she was able to persuade him to accompany her and the baby down the dark stairs.

Once in the high-domed chamber, she pulled him from one place to another, demonstrating its wonders. She showed him the three large stones in the center, the suspended rubies, the panel of jewels, the bronze mirror. These he could see and accept. But when Tinker looked in the mirror, he could not see what she saw. He could not see any of the vast throng of women Clever-Lazy described so clearly.

"Look! Look!" she kept saying to him. Then, in exasperation, "Oh, Tinker, I do expect that the important things of life we see the same way."

"I can't see something that's not there," said Tinker.

Clever-Lazy's cheeks flamed dangerously. "Are you saying I'm not telling the truth?"

"I am saying you are telling *your* truth. Not mine."

"Tinker, listen to me. I see the Goddess and I see that she is made up of all my bits and pieces. Right now I can even see you and Noisemaker added in the mirror so you are part of my Goddess, too. But you don't have to see and believe the same thing. You'll invent your own truth."

"What happens when we agree?" asked Tinker, bewildered.

"That's wonderful."

"And if we don't?"

She paused. "Then it can't be helped."

She flung her arms around him. "Oh, Tinker! You aren't in this world to do what I expect of you. And I'm not here to be respectable." Then Clever-Lazy laughed.

What Tinker heard was not a girlish giggle but a woman's laugh, throaty and rich and full of joy.

Clever-Lazy's guess that the whistle would open all three doors proved to be right. They made several trips to bring all their belongings through the passageway to the first door she had entered to get into the mountain. When she blew a high, piercing squeal, it opened onto the ledge where she and Noisemaker had spent those miserable hours trapped in cold mist and rain. Now they could see their way clearly as Tinker followed her along the path toward the base of the cliff. They passed the waterfall, descended through the woods to the valley and found their home, snug and dear, waiting for them.

Late in the evening, when Noisemaker was sleeping peacefully, Clever-Lazy and Tinker lay on a skin rug spread at one corner of the mosaic. A tallow lamp set shadows flickering on walls and floor.

"The mountains really *are* dancing!" marveled Clever-Lazy, touching the mauve-colored prisms that rose out of green hills. "And do look! Here is the river going to the Southeast Sea, and here are towers and pleasure domes of the Emperor's capital. Here are miles of fertile ground, and here is the marsh filled with sinuous rills and incense-bearing trees. Why, it's like a map of all the places we had to go through to get here. Surely the Goddess brought you and me and Noisemaker here for a purpose."

"But why? And how? What does it all mean?" asked Tinker.

"I don't know why, or even how," said Clever-Lazy.

Then she reached out a fingertip and traced the blazing head, the shimmering lengths of the dragon as it floated in the depths of an incredible sky.